WHEN IS THE

First Lady

ever

FIRST

BARBARA J. WARREN MCKINNEY

PRESS

Foreword
By
Bishop George Dallas McKinney

*B*arbara J. Warren McKinney's book is a clear demonstration of the power of fiction to capture and portray truth and reality in such a way to encourage godly thinking and behavior. The author has written a book that is thoroughly entertaining. The reader is allowed to experience vicariously the life of a "First Lady," her family and her peers. At the same time, in each chapter, there is a presentation of different critical life situations, challenges, and moral dilemmas that draws the reader into this exciting story.

The book provides an insider's view of the sub-culture in the mega church charismatic, Pentecostal movement. While the main characters are successful, they nevertheless, are confronted with the problem and issues common to all of us. The characters wrestle with the real life problems of depression, suicide, abortion, marital infidelity, homosexuality, and hypoc-risy. From the opening paragraph to the conclusion there is a clear biblical emphasis on maintaining healthy relationships by practicing love and forgiveness. In Chapter 15, the ulti-mate price of unforgiveness is separation from God and broken human relationships.

Since 2008, the author has served as the "First Lady" at St. Stephen's Church Of God In Christ with her husband. She fulfills this role with true spirituality, dignity, and compassion. Barbara McKinney 's spiritual journey and career path began in Wichita Kansas. She committed her life to Christ at an early age. She earned a BS Degree at the University of Kansas in Pittsburg, Kansas, a Master's degree in Public Administration at the University of Missouri, and a Juris Doctorate degree from the University of Notre Dame.

The author has served as legal counsel to a number of churches; she practiced law in Dallas for over 30 years. She served as the first African American and female judge of the Municipal Court in Waxahachie Texas. She is now part of the legal staff of the Church Of God In Christ.

I am proud to recommend this book to all of the first ladies of the world and to the general public, especially those who are committed to seeing first ladies as equal members of the ministry team.

Dedication

This book is dedicated to the love of my life, Bishop George
Dallas McKinney, who has supported this endeavor since
its inception. His walk with God and commitment to me has
been an inspiration and source of great strength.
I extend this dedication to all the first ladies, who have
committed their lives to Ministry. May God continue to
strengthen you for the journey.

In Grateful Acknowledgment

 want to thank God for giving me the insight and courage to put pen to paper. God has been good to me. He has always been with me and has never failed me.

I thank the love of my life that supported me every step of the way, and for his thoughtful foreword to this book, my husband, George.

I shall always be indebted to Joy (Dabbs) and Shanetha (Buchanan) who started this brainstorming journey with me in 2012.

I pray God's blessings on Wendy (McKinney) who helped me during my finals days, encouraging me to finish the book.

I shall always be thankful to Traci (Wooden- Carlisle) for her contributions in editing, proofing and her creativity, a tremendous writer.

Finally, I can't thank Louie (Lee), Jamillah (Lee) and Eliana (Lee) enough for putting up with me night and day for the last year in trying to get to this place.

Table of Contents

CHAPTER 1

The Most Perfect Day

The beginning of the End

This was the most perfect day. The palm trees swayed against the light breeze, and every imaginable flower was planted perfectly in the ground. Some of the flowers looked like they were plucked right out of African rich soil; such was the vibrancy of their colors. The yellows, purples, reds and various shades of blue cast a feeling of otherworldliness on the warm Miami day. The long-limbed trees were everywhere, all shapes and sizes, bending gracefully in the wind. This place looked like paradise on earth. Words could hardly describe the beauty of this place, with its meticulously manicured, emerald colored lawns and the perfect planting of flowers and these majestic palm trees. It was simply breathtaking.

As I gazed to my right, I saw a white carriage trimmed in gold being pulled by six white, prancing horses; their long hair seemed to wave as they slowed to a trot along the narrow road lined with even more flowers. It was such a splendid sight, but then I realized this place of beauty, this paradise, was a cemetery, and this white carriage trimmed in gold was carrying a casket.

Even with this realization I couldn't help but notice that the flowers seemed to stand at attention; the clarity of color in them lost to the occupant of the carriage. All of this beauty and splendor, from flowers, to trees, to the rolling greens that rivaled the best country clubs in the nation. The ones that spent the most time here would never see their perfect hues or partake of their fragrances. All this beauty is for the dead, and those who mourn them.

Very rarely was so much attention given to a funeral for the wife of a religious figure. The 16,000-seat church was filled to capacity and within minutes of the doors opening it became standing room only with a crowd of people standing outside. Very few media personnel were allowed inside, but just beyond the perimeter set for those who came to give their respects was the crush of media vans, reporters, videographers, and photographers.

I knew that The True Way Trinity Church was the largest non-denominational church in Miami, Florida, where Jane and

Ron Steinbeck ministered to 30,000 members each Sunday between two services. It was also the largest TV ministry broadcast on a major network in the United States. I'd known the Steinbecks since before they began their ministry over twenty-five years ago. Even before they began their TV ministry, which was still going strong after ten years, they were considered one of the most successful ministries in the country.

As I sat amongst the sea of black and gray attired mourners, I never felt as insignificant as I did at that moment, and True Way Trinity Church had never felt so cold and detached. It was located close to the downtown area and with parking it covered nearly four city blocks. The sanctuary was set up like a theatre so that no matter where you were seated you could see the pulpit. There were ten doors to the outside and security for the funeral covered every door. Some of the streets were blocked off going into the downtown area. The police who were directing the enclave to the cemetery were members of the congregation. A large population of the Miami Police Department actually attended the church, so they were out in full force.

Ron, Jane's husband, had been in law enforcement before he went into fulltime ministry, and had dedicated his entire professional career to law enforcement. It was apparent through the massive turnout of police officers that even after retirement he'd maintained close friendships and camaraderie with many of his former co-workers. There must have been at least fifty police cars and anywhere from thirty to fifty motorcycle policemen.

Although the church was closed to most of the media, the upscale Golden Gate Cemetery where Jane's interment took place, was a totally different story. The narrow roads winding through the Golden Gate Cemetery from Main Street were completely jam packed with limousines and cars. Everybody who was somebody in the church world was there: pastors and first ladies from other countries, a representative from every major ministry in this country, even the Vice President of the United States was in attendance.

Though they were held back for security reasons, even Pastor Steinbeck's impassioned plea couldn't keep every major media source from sending at least one representative to the cemetery.

The news of Jane's death had flashed across my television screen barely hours after I had been notified, and I could only watch in horror as speculations and allegations were reported on the BNC network. Reporters and commentators were talking about the possibility of Jane Steinbeck, the wife of this TV Evangelist, taking her own life. My eyes burned with indignation at the spectacle and circus they were making of Jane's memorial. There were all kinds of speculation as to what happened and whether it could have been avoided.

Terry Akin of BNC was interviewing pastors of other large congregations as they tried to make their way from their vehicles to the interment site. When he could no longer get answers from them, he moved on. I saw him later that evening, on his nightly news show, asking what I could only guess was opinions from a few well-known psychologists. They couldn't have known what happened, so they were theorizing on what happened. As a psychologist and a long time friend of Jane's, I knew it would only be a matter of time before Terry Akin would ask me for an interview.

As I made my way closer to the site, I heard whispers ranging from the possibility of foul play, to some type of scandal in the first family, to outside forces trying to get at the pastor, and of course, the possibility of suicide.

Terry Akin characterized the activity at the cemetery as media frenzy. At least he had that right, frenzy was the perfect word.

Lisa Payne, Jane Steinbeck's personal assistant, shared with me the events of that unforgettable Sunday, through tears I listened intently. I wondered what must have been going through my best friend's mind. I imagined it was more than a normal day with their megachurch on TV with spotlights going back and forth, shining over the crowd, in that huge arena with about 15,000 people. I recalled on the Sunday mornings I would attend, the praise team would sing, raising the praise and worship level to that of pandemonium. The cameras, which I was never able to get use to, were panning back and forth over the congregation. That Sunday morning, Lisa explained that she knocked on the door as usual, walked in and said, "First Lady, you have five minutes." First Lady Jane nodded her head, never turning around and said, "I will be right out."

Lisa noticed First Lady Jane was writing, and a bottle of pills was next to her papers on the desk.

Lisa continued to explain, "Church was about over, and I did not see First Lady come out of her office, but that was not unusual because she did not typically sit on stage with Pastor Ron. She liked greeting the people; she could have been in the vestibule or she could have gone directly to the balcony; she did that a lot."

We all knew Pastor Ron always acknowledged her while on stage and asked her to stand, wherever she was, but this particular Sunday he didn't do that. In fact, this was the first time Lisa said she could recall him not acknowledging her since she'd been at True Way Trinity.

"When church was over, I waited at the stage," Lisa continued, "because First Lady Jane usually came to the stage after church and greeted the people with Pastor Ron, but this Sunday she did not come to the stage."

I touched Lisa's hand when it looked as though she wouldn't be able to finish but she regained some of her composure and explained, "Pastor Ron greeted members of the congregation for almost forty-five minutes, as he did every Sunday, but this Sunday he greeted the members alone.

After he had finished greeting the people, he asked me if I had seen Lady Jane. I explained that I hadn't seen her during the service. He asked me to tell First Lady to meet him in the dining room because they'd planned to stay at church for dinner.

Pastor Ron looked exhausted; this was the last service for the day. I told him I would escort Lady Jane to the dining hall.

I figured Lady Jane must have gone back to her office, so I went to Lady Jane's office and knocked on the door, but there was no answer. I called out to her, but there was no answer."

The tears began to slide down Lisa's cheeks.

"I went to open the door but it was locked, which was highly unusual because Lady Jane never locked her door. I became very worried because I did not have the key with me, so I had one of the security personnel open the door. Once he opened it; I thanked him, grabbed the door, and closed it right behind me because I didn't know what to expect."

I watched as Lisa's face crumpled and my heart felt every sob that came from her throat. I reached for her hand and tried to convey my appreciation for what she was doing and comforted her for what it was costing her to relive these moments.

When her tears no longer stood in the way of her voice she spoke. At first it was choppy as if she was trying to distance herself from her words, but then they began to flow.

"Inside the room I found Lady Jane slumped over her desk. I panicked and called security, who was still right outside the door. When he came in, the guard saw Lady Jane was unconscious and tried to resuscitate her, but to no avail. I called for Pastor Ron and the paramedics. By the time Pastor Ron arrived at the room, First Lady appeared lifeless. The paramedics were there within minutes; they also attempted to resuscitate her and proceeded to rush her to the hospital.

I was distraught. I went to the hospital with some friends and waited until they officially announced First Lady Jane's death." Lisa shook her head. "I was studying to be a nurse and had taken Lady Jane's pulse before she left the church. It was very weak, and I knew there was a good chance she wouldn't make it to the hospital.

I sat outside of Lady Jane's hospital room for at least two hours, crying quietly. When Pastor Ron and Bryan left the room with the chaplain after the first hour and tried to get me to leave, I told them I would be leaving soon. I wasn't sure if I meant it.

When I finally left the room, all I could think about was my first lady was gone, and I didn't know why."

Lisa stared down at the floor lost in thought for a moment; I had to call her name to nudge her back to the story she was telling.

"All of my training as an assistant to the first lady made me confident of my responsibility and obligation to Lady Jane. My assignment was a lifetime assignment, to assist her all the way to the grave. I had heard it discussed in our training, but never did it carry so much meaning as it did at that moment.

I asked the nurse if I could go back into the room to make sure Lady Jane's hair was okay; that her eyes were closed, and just for a last look. I explained to her that I was Mrs. Steinbeck's personal assistant. The nurses were very kind and allowed me to go back into the room. As I looked at Lady Jane, I thought about her favorite color and how I would dress First Lady for the funeral, hat and all. I noticed Lady Jane still had her wedding band on her finger. I removed the ring, knowing the pastor would want it, and checked Lady Jane for any other jewelry. I made sure her eyes were closed, and I left the room."

As Lisa was sharing the events of what happened, the ringing of the telephone brought me out of my thoughts. I reached over to silence the ring tone. I was miffed with myself for not muting my phone. I always silenced my phone when meeting clients in my office, that's part of my protocol, but Lisa was not a client. I never cry with clients, but Lisa and I couldn't stop crying.

Jane had a relatively small family and Ron said he wanted the funeral to take place as soon as possible. Ron had contacted the other children; they were a very close-knit family. There were four children; Ron, Jr. is the oldest with a wife, Mary and two children, Ron Steinbeck, III and Lilly, living in Tampa Florida. Ron, Jr. has been away from home for the last ten years. He had a great relationship with his parents, and he was also a Pastor. Then there was Stacy, who couldn't seem to leave home fast enough. She had always been headstrong and determined. She was a recent graduate of Miami University and lived in Tampa, and attended her brother Ron, Jr.'s church. She was a political science major. Their youngest daughter, Madeline, was also single and away at school attending Cornell University. She was working on a degree in computer science. Although she was a daddy's girl, I recall her mother telling me how close they had always been; the long mother-daughter talks over midnight dessert would never be again. Bryan, seventeen, was the only child at home.

Another reason Ron did not want to prolong the funeral was because the news of Jane's death was on television almost every day, and reporters were trying to talk to him daily. They were speculating that maybe there was foul play. I was told that the police had interviewed Ron about what was going on in the household.

When I asked Ron myself what happened, late that Tuesday night, he appeared to be holding something back, something he didn't want to share, and if the police noticed the same thing I did, I'm sure they thought it looked very suspicious. I asked him several times if he had any idea why she would want to take her life, trying to find any piece of information I could that would help explain the huge puzzle sitting before me, and he continued to say he did not know. The family had certain secrets that were not shared with anyone, but Ron didn't think anything he knew would cause her to take her life. I wasn't surprised when he told me that the police did not believe him; they continued to investigate her death and said they would keep the case open until they gathered more information.

I wish I'd thrown away the newspaper. The few pleasant words said in the article were clearly overshadowed by allegations. I moved the paper to the edge of my desk, unintentionally uncovering the program from Jane's funeral service, and

I was once again zipping back in time through my mind's eye experiencing the funeral all over again.

When I learned Lisa was given the responsibility of preparing Jane, selecting her dress and the accessories, I was relieved to know that she was still up to the task and that Jane's body was going to be prepared by someone who knew her well. With Lisa also on the committee that was to prepare for the funeral, the programs, the guest list, and the seating chart, I felt more than confident that I could take the time to mourn.

The main sanctuary was open to general seating. It was first come, first serve for members of the church, along with two other areas where only members would be allowed to view the funeral on-screen. There were some media invited to the funeral, but no cameras were permitted.

As I sat in the row reserved for the family, my hand tightly encased in my husband's hand, I could feel the suffocating weight of the atmosphere all around. Jane's funeral was so sad. It's different when you're sick and you take a turn for the worse and die, but this was a vibrant, beautiful woman that was loved by everyone. Many envied her; she had a wonderful life, a wonderful home, and was the First Lady to a tremendous church.

Funerals in Jane's church were known as Home Going Celebrations, but there was nothing celebratory about Jane's funeral. I'd attended several funerals at Jane's church due to us sharing a lot of the same acquaintances. We knew a few of the same people, even with us leading different churches, caring for people took up a significant amount of our lives and we knew quite a few of the same people.

The programs for her church were always entitled "Home Going Celebration," but not Jane's program, it said, "Our Beloved Jane Will Be Missed." The actual program even looked sad. I couldn't help wondering if "Home Going Celebration" was purposely left off the program. There were two pictures on the front; one of Jane and one of her family.

There were only two songs sung, though I remembered how much Jane loved music. The service was exactly one hour, including the procession into the sanctuary and the recession out of the sanctuary. The church was filled to capacity. Knowing that all of the members could not fit in the sanctuary, the family and leadership decided to hold two services to accommodate the crowd. Even the gym and banquet room were set up with rows of seating and large screens to act as an overflow for as many members as possible. Many of the members began lining up outside two hours before the service. Everyone, including those outside, in the gym and the banquet hall, were allowed to view the body. Jane was simply beautiful. Her assistant, Lisa, dressed her in a beautiful white dress with a lovely hat.

Though the program was not long; ten people talked and were allowed two minutes each. They represented the clergy, pastors' wives, members of the church, and family members. Since the Mayor of Miami was a friend of Ron and Jane's, he was allowed more time to speak. The Mayor was very personable in his delivery. He shared so many personal thoughts about Jane, it was obvious he knew her well.

Sadness hung heavy in the air. Many people were crying, but at the same time, it was a beautiful service. The casket was white, trimmed in gold, surrounded by hundreds of beautiful flowers. When the funeral was over, and people were processioned out of the church, there was very little greeting or speaking. I saw a number of people I knew. I smiled, occasionally, but I never opened my mouth to speak.

Everyone was moving quietly out of the sanctuary. My husband, son, and I walked quietly to our car and lined up for the procession to the cemetery. Once I sat down in the car, I just lost it; I broke down and openly cried out. This was my friend, who I thought shared everything with me. I was crying because my best friend was gone. I was crying because my best friend betrayed me. I was crying because I was angry and confused, and didn't know what really happened to cause my friend to take her own life.

As we got closer to the Golden Gate Cemetery, I regained my composure. It wasn't that far, but the procession was so long it took about an hour to drive there. My husband had a special flag from the funeral home on our car, which allowed us to be toward the front of the procession. As we turned onto the cemetery grounds, it was very obvious, with all of the cars and TV trucks already on the cemetery grounds; a majority of the procession would not be able to enter. The media vehicles didn't take away any space from the cars in the procession, but the procession was so long many parked alongside the cemeteries outside gate and walked in.

As I got out of the car and began to walk to the mausoleum, I got all choked up again and wanted to go back to the car, but I didn't. I continued to walk towards where the family was sitting.

I knew the media would be present, but I had no idea so many media people would be there. Mr. Akins of BCN and someone from Liberty News had already interviewed me. I had been interviewed in these types of situations before. It seems they are always looking for a psychologist to discuss what would make a person commit suicide.

The media knew that Jane and I were good friends, and I was acquainted with most of them because of my many interviews on local and national matters. Due to my specific discipline as a psychologist, I'd dealt with many well-known people who had taken their life. Akins had interviewed me three times in the past and the request for my commentary, I knew, was to gain professional and personal insight into Jane's actions. But, as I explained to him, I was just as shocked as everybody else. I explained that I didn't have a clue what happened to Jane. Although we were close, nothing I knew could have prepared me for her taking her life.

At the Golden Gate Cemetery, Jane's assistant, Lisa, walked over to me and attempted to hand me a sealed letter, but I was crying and so grief-stricken that Lisa asked my son, Jake, who was standing nearby, to receive the letter for me. He later told me that she placed the envelope in his hand and had him promise to give it to me unopened once we left the cemetery. Jake agreed.

He said Lisa made it very clear the document was very important, and for my eyes-only.

After the graveside service, I walked over to Ron, Bryan, and the other family members and hugged them.

When Jonathan, Jake, and I got back in the limo, Jake laid the envelope in my lap and told me it was from Lisa, Mrs. Steinbeck's personal assistant. I said, "What is it?" I looked closely at it and said, "Never mind." I knew the handwriting. I just held it close to my chest and didn't say another word in the limo to anybody. I didn't know how to feel. The thought that she had left me a letter made me a little excited, but when considering what I might find in that letter I was struck with fear, and both of these new emotions combined with the gut-wrenching grief left me with no energy to exorcise them.

In my quiet time, later that day, I reflected back on those who were at the cemetery; so many people. I flashed back to the faces of some of the first ladies that were there. Some were crying profusely; others were shaking their heads; one was hiding her tears, holding her head really high as if she was above all of this, looking as if she was the queen of England, but she was the one that seemed to be hurting the most.

As I sat in my easy chair with tears running down my cheeks, I began to think and retrace the steps in my relationship with Jane. *Why didn't I see it coming? How did I miss this? I am trained to detect someone with suicidal tendencies. Jane and I talked almost every day, and neither depression nor suicide was ever discussed.*

I needed some answers before I opened this letter. If I'd been in any shape to do so at the cemetery, I would have gotten answers as soon as Lisa handed the letter to my son.

I picked up the phone and called Lisa. She picked up the line after the third ring. "Yes, First Lady Eckles." She answered.

"I received the letter you handed to my son."

Silence was her answer.

"I have some questions for you."

"Have you read the letter?", Lisa Responded.

"Not yet. Can you come by?" There was a slight pause then I heard her sigh.

"When?"

"As soon as possible."

"I will be there in an hour."

"Very good. Thank you Lisa." I said relieved.

"Goodbye." She said quietly, and then disconnected the call.

I knew Lisa was tired when she first walked through my door, but the need for answers overrode my compassion at the moment. After offering her something to eat and drink, I jumped right into questioning her about how she'd come about the letter that was now in my hands.

Lisa began to explain, "I had left my purse and other personal belongings at the church, when I went to the hospital. I

26

had one of my friends take take me back to the church to pick them up. I went to my office, and as I approached my belongings, I saw a manila envelope on top of my purse with a note. 'This is confidential Lisa' was written on the side facing up. Upon recognizing Lady Jane's handwriting, my already frayed nerves sent jolts of alarm through my system. Attached to the folder was a letter to me."

Lisa retrieved the letter from her purse and handed it to me. I slowly unfolded the note and began reading out loud.

"Please keep the whole package until my funeral, and then give the inside envelope to my dear friend Mary Eckles, at the gravesite. Please do not open the envelope; the sealed letter is for Mary's eyes only.

Thank you for being the best assistant I have ever had. Please continue to help the ministry and my husband. If you will look in your top drawer, I put a letter in there for my husband as well. Please hold onto his sealed letter and give it to him no earlier than five days after the funeral.

Lisa, we have had a great journey together. In my letter to my husband, I asked him to share some things with you because of the help you have been to me. You are like my own daughter. I really want you to understand what I know to be my only option. In time, my husband will talk with you, and share some things that I have kept secret for over 22 years.

I pray that you have much happiness. I have made some terrible mistakes. I pray that you are very careful in life, and always stay close to the church and the church mothers. I didn't do that, and it became harder and harder to share my problems. Don't make my mistakes. Please forgive me.

Love You Dearly,
Jane"

As I looked up at Lisa, words cannot describe the pain I saw in her eyes.

Lisa was holding onto the letter for Ron and really wanted to give it to him right away, but Jane had told her to wait until five days after the funeral. Lisa felt it might be helpful in understanding Jane's death. She was concerned because the police kept meeting with Ron. The police asked Ron if Jane had left a note prior to her death. Ron kept telling them Jane didn't leave anything. Lisa felt very uncomfortable because three notes were left: one for her, one for me, and one for Ron. Nobody asked her about a note, so she felt she didn't have to volunteer this information. When she asked me why Jane would have her keep the letters until a certain time, the ideas raced through my mind, being rejected faster than I could truly acknowledge them, but there was one that stuck. "Maybe Jane knew there would be a lot of questions from authorities and didn't want them to get their hands on these notes." Lisa decided she did not want to turn the notes over to the police because Jane talked about a secret she had kept for 22 years. It was not her place to open that up, but Ron certainly could do it. Jane did say she asked Ron to share with Lisa what they had concealed for so many years.

After Lisa left, I stared at the letter lying on my desk for a long time, knowing I would be held accountable for the knowledge I gained from Jane's words. I took a deep breath and reached for it.

As I began to read the manuscript that Jane had meticulously put together, I thought about what was going on in her mind regarding taking her life and why she was so preoccupied in the letter with helping a group of first ladies. Were they going through what she was going through? I had known Jane for *over twenty-five years*, and I could not for the life of me figure out what happened. I continued to read her letter with eager anticipation in hopes she would share what caused her to take her life.

Jane took a lot of time to write this letter to me for a reason, and that weighed heavy on my heart. I started reading Jane's letter all over again.

"Dear Mary,

You have been my friend for over two and a half decades. You have always been there for me, and we have shared wonderful memories together. I wish I had opened up more to you, I really wanted to. I guess I didn't want you to think I was weak-minded and not able to handle being the first lady, but it was so much more than just being first lady. I wish people understood our life doesn't start and stop with being first lady; our lives are so much broader, deeper and more compli-cated than the responsibilities of our position.

The first lady certainly has important responsibilities. One of the most important responsibilities is that she undergirds her husband and supports his vision. She is to lead the women in supporting his vision. Mary, we deal with other things as well (smile). The first lady also deals with people who smile in her face, watching her every move, while they wait for her to make a mistake. They are clearly, watching to see what she is wearing when she walks into the church, and whether she will have on a hat or not. Your stockings, oh yes, they are going to check out your stockings and make sure you don't have a run. If you have one, that's a discussion. (Smile) Mary, we have had some great laughs together and great memories; I have enjoyed our friendship.

Remember how the women seemed to fall all over our husbands, smiling at us, and looking at our husbands all at the same time? (smile)

It was difficult early in our marriage because I think Pastor got caught up with one of the members. I never let him know I knew, but I did. He finally got himself together and severed that relationship, but she remains a part of our congregation in an intricate way; he still depends on her today. That's okay because I know he's moved on.

Mary, this is a hard life. The lonely nights, feeling like I had no friends, and not knowing who to trust. So many people around me, yet I was so all alone. You don't have a life of your own; you are first lady. That's your life, and everybody is looking at you to do everything right. My life encompasses so much more than being the first lady. I am a human being who is so tired of being so many things to so many people. I hurt; I cry; I want to be comforted. Who comforts me? I need someone I can share my worst fears along with the heartache I feel in the pit of my stomach that never goes away; who tells me, "I got you; it's going to be all right." Mary, don't get me wrong, I have faith. God knows, I have tried to hold onto my faith, trusting in Him, but I am so tired.

I want you to do me a favor, a big favor. First ladies need help; they need to know there is someone who understands that although they are first ladies, they are individuals with real needs that go beyond first lady duties. They need to be validated. We are all going through so much; some of the husbands are treating their wives as fixtures, something pretty to sit on the shelf, and then take them down when it's time to show them off. Some never acknowledge the contributions of the first lady and the intricate role she plays in the ministry. Mary, I didn't have these problems, but I knew they existed among some of my friends.

Mary, if you do anything, reach out to these women. That is my desire from you. Reach out and do what only you can do. So many need your help, if you could help these ladies and their families, you would honor my memory.

You will have to talk to them in depth, but I want to share a little bit about each of them. There is a young lady, Plessey Humphrey, that I really don't know, but she is a friend of one of my friends, Elona Braggs. Elona shared some things about this family, and they need help as well. Please talk to Elona about Plessey. Mary, I know you can't help the whole world but if you would take

*some time to work with these ladies and their families,
I would be grateful.*

*First, there is Pastor Terri, a powerful woman of God.
I am not sure what's going on in their marriage. I
believe, but I don't know for sure, her husband, Pastor
Larry, is physically abusing her. There is some kind of
abuse taking place; maybe it's mental abuse. Please do
what you can to help Pastor Terri; she lives in Miami
Beach, not far from their beautiful church, St. Mark
Ministries. She and Pastor Larry built the church about
four years ago.*

*The second young lady is Patricia Harris, who is an
attorney in Houston, Texas. She and her husband come
every year to our conference, and we have been good
friends for at least ten years. I don't think she has
the problem, I think it's her husband, but it really is
affecting the ministry. The people love Pastor Patricia,
but I don't think her husband is happy about the attention his wife gets from the church. She is a great speaker
but he very seldom allows her to speak in church. The
insecurity is so severe on his part it could destroy the
marriage and the ministry. Mary you and I have spent
a lot of time talking about Patricia and you know the
problems she faces.*

Evangelist Elona Braggs is a dear friend of mine. She is English and lives in London; she is not a First Lady. I know you know her because everybody knows her powerful ministry in London and in the US; she suffers from depression. She has done some things, and it has been hard for her to forgive herself. I am really worried about her; she is at her wit's end.

Please don't forget to talk with her about Plessey Humphrey.

Mary, thank you for all you have done for me, and what you are about to do for my friends. I know my decision for my life is an extreme one; I just don't want this to happen to any of my friends. Please don't judge me, I just want to get off this merry-go-round; I just can't go around again. If I thought things could get better, this would not be an option, but I have thought long and hard about what I am about to do, and for me this is the only option. There is no other way for me. The pain I am experiencing is too much to bear.

I love my family, and I am sure they love me, but they will get along just fine without me.

I love you, Mary, for your faithfulness and your strength.
Please reach out to help my sisters in the ministry, as
they are all hurting. If anybody can reach them, you can.

Our lives as first ladies are not supposed to be like this,
Mary. Is the First Lady ever first? How is she first?
Who put her first? I know there is an element of respect
that comes with being the first lady, but there is also
a responsibility that's placed on the first lady to earn
that respect.

Mary, is it just a fancy name [smile] what does
it all mean?

Love you,
Jane

As I came back to awareness of myself, I realized I was
clutching my blouse with hand fisted over my heart. I literally
hurt for my friend, for myself, and for these women who, if I
could, I would help as recompense for not being able to save
my best friend.

CHAPTER 2

The Silent Tears

Are we Listening?

Flashback on conversations between Mary and Jane

"Mary, have you ever felt you wanted to get away from it all?"

Jane said that to me all the time, but I didn't think anything about it. When she'd say she wanted us to take a trip together, I would say, "Sure; you're busier than I am, we would never have time to do that."

Jane asked me several times to go out to dinner during the last month, but we could never get our schedules to line up. She had never been so persistent before then; she was always the busy one, never really had time. As I reflected back on our conversations, it seemed as if she was trying to make time. I couldn't see it then, but now I see she was reaching out to me for help. "Oh my God, forgive me for not being there."

Sometimes, we get so busy and preoccupied with our own little world, we appear to be listening, but we are really going through the motions of listening. We have to care more about each other and be sensitive towards one another and truly listen. There is no way to get the true meaning of what someone is trying to say if you are not really listening. It's important to practice active listening to hear and process what's being said. If I had really listened to Jane, I would have clearly known she was reaching out to me. It wasn't that I wasn't listening to the conversation, but I was only listening to the point of being able to respond to what was being said. I didn't give much thought to the fact that what Jane was saying, was really out of character, but if I had been truly listening, I would have realized she was crying out for my full attention.

Jane lived in a house with her husband and 17-year-old son, Bryan. Couldn't they see something was wrong? I wanted to ask Ron so bad, what was going on in that house? Why didn't he detect something was wrong? Was Jane that invisible that nobody noticed her? Jane was always concerned about the welfare of others. She was a giver, of her time, her love, and her money; there was nothing she wouldn't do for anyone. Jane was the kind of person, if you were a beggar on the street and you greeted her, she would stretch out her hand to shake your hand. She was amazing. I knew Jane was always there for others, but it seemed nobody was there for her.

I remember Jane sharing with me after one particularly busy afternoon, "It's lonely being the first lady, so many responsibilities and so many people depend on you. You share their hurts, and their concerns about ministry. They express a desire to be more active in the church; they share their concerns of being overlooked by leadership. They share concerns about how dysfunctional their family has become. They request prayer, a hug, a kiss, and a need to be recognized by the First Family. Multiply that by 300 or 400 or even 1,000, and in my case, 30,000." She blew out a weary sigh. "You must appear strong, with wide shoulders to lean on, to cry on. Although it is impossible to reach out and connect with everybody, you feel this pull to do just that. You want members to know the First Family loves them.

When you have ended your Sunday service and you have given your last smile, your last hug, your last kiss, your last 'we love you and we are praying for you,' you go home, take off your Sunday best, sit down in your easy chair, and then let out a sigh of relief. Sometimes, it only takes a smile, a hug, or a kiss to make someone's life a little brighter, and at that moment you know, God is pleased."

I smiled that knowing smile at her because I knew exactly how she felt – on a smaller scale, of course.

I can't begin to describe how truly amazing Jane was with people. Jane once told me the greatness of this journey was the people and being positioned to love and serve the people.

She met no stranger, yet she felt like a stranger in her own surroundings.

I looked at Jane's letter again, touching the pages as if I could feel my friend in them or at least catch a bit of her essence. "I wonder if she was writing this to me at that moment." I thought absentmindedly, smoothing my hands over the words explaining the pain, loneliness, and complete emptiness that had developed over the past couple of years. "Why didn't you say something?" I whispered into the stillness of the room. "We had so many things in common. I could have helped you." I pushed the letter away from me; afraid I would wet it with the tears that sprang free due to my pensive reflections. I glanced at a picture of the four of us on my desk. It had been taken during a pastors and wives retreat. Jane and I had long talks surrounding the expectations of being pastors' wives. I thought she knew she could talk with me about anything, even if it meant taking off my professional hat as a psychologist.

As I continued to look around my office, my eyes fell upon a picture of Jane and Ron posing outside one of the Pastors' Conferences in Dallas. Jane could turn on that smile with a second's notice. She loved to take pictures.

In the midst of all she was going through, her thoughts were on others; she didn't want anyone else to experience what she was feeling. Her last wish, her last desire, was for first ladies to get the help they needed. She knew they needed help because of where she was mentally. Her desire was for me to reach out and help them. I can't even begin to put my arms around where she was mentally—what was pulling her so strong.

Jane was a woman of faith. She taught Bible study, and she was a student of the word. When she prayed, everyone who heard her felt the anointing on her life; she had a gift that could only come from God. She always had a kind word, whether you sat on the front row or up in the balcony. She treated everyone the same.

Ron used to tell me; sometimes, during service he couldn't find Jane. She didn't have any particular seat; she very seldom sat on the stage with Ron. Instead, she would be all over the place; she would be sitting somewhere down with the audience. Ron would often say, "My wife is here. Stand up, honey, and wave your hand." Jane would stand up from a different place every Sunday, waving both hands with that million-dollar smile. Many times you would find Jane up in the balcony. She wanted to experience what others' were experiencing wherever they sat.

When church was over, sometimes you would see Jane walking down the stairs from the balcony with someone who looked like they might have just walked off the street. She would have that beautiful smile spread across her face like she just met the President. She made people feel special as if they were so important. She listened to their problems and she literally cried with members. She felt their pain, their loneliness. When she would embrace you, it didn't matter who you were—it was warm, it was real, and you felt special.

Jane was a good friend. The question I ask myself, and the question I ask God, was WHY?

Why did she take her life? Why didn't Ron and her son Bryan hear or see the signs? I was close to Jane's girls, Stacy and Madeline. We talked just about every week. They never mentioned Jane was having problems. They knew how close Jane was to me. If they had known, they would have shared with me any problems Jane was having.

Why didn't her assistant, Lisa, who she talked with everyday, notice something was different?

Why didn't I detect something was wrong? We talked daily. As I think about some of her recent conversations, I guess there were signs I just didn't pick up on, because this was my friend that had it all together.

There were so many good things about Jane, yet there was a dark side that nobody knew; there had to be—she killed herself.

As I considered that thought more and more, I replayed encounters and conversations we had with a different perspective. One particular event came to mind, making it crystal clear that I had witnessed my friend's subtle changes, but allowed myself to be appeased by her denials.

At her husband's, 55th birthday party that everyone was invited to, Jane seemed so happy and excited, but I remember at times she seemed not to be there at all. She was talking, she was engaging, but something about her led me to believe she was far away. I just don't know what it could have been. I've seen that look before with Jane; I would ask her what she was thinking about, and she would snap back and say, "Oh nothing, just thinking."

So, now, I have this awesome task of reaching out to a group of first ladies who appear to be strong, totally together, with awesome ministries. How do I begin this journey? I don't have a choice; it is something I must do. Only God can lead me in the right direction, and only God can give me the words to say.

I remember many of the first ladies from the cemetery, including those women whose names Jane shared in her letter.

I remember Amy Hemphill, who has a very prominent TV ministry along with her husband. She was crying profusely. It is hard to describe what I saw. Though it wasn't the cry of losing your best friend; her tears were personal, as if they were coming from deep inside. At one point, she even looked as if she wanted to scream—it was the strangest look. She was crying so uncontrollably, it was if she couldn't help it. I could tell she wasn't concerned with who saw her tears, but what *was* strange she wasn't making a sound. Her husband was standing by her side but didn't seem to notice. You know how two people are together, but their body language reflects something different? That's what I remember most of all, their body language toward one another or rather the distance from one another.

I then looked across the crowd and saw Pastor Terri Jones, the wife of Pastor Larry Jones, who has a megachurch in Florida. He is an African American pastor who has taken ministry to a whole new level. He has a TV ministry, a movie production company, and a well-known travel agency that everybody uses.

His ministry is in South Florida where his beautiful church sits almost on the water, surrounded by palm trees. I have attended their services a couple of times with my husband. When you are sitting in the sanctuary, you can look out the window and see nothing but water.

Well, getting back to Pastor Terri—she's a tall, beautiful, middle-aged lady who is somewhat self-made. She is poised and very refined. Terri does not have a formal education, as she jumped right into ministry with her husband and never took the time to go to college, but you wouldn't know it. Pastor Terri is an avid reader. She loves the symphony and the opera and has season tickets to both.

She and her husband have a television ministry, and she shared her story of not having a formal education during one of their TV shows. She also talked about her love for the symphony and the opera.

Pastor Terri seemed very sad as I looked back during the funeral services. I know she knew Jane personally; they were good friends. I don't recall her crying—she just seemed very sad.

Elona Braggs, the well-known TV evangelist from London, was there with her entourage. When she has appointments in the United States, the tickets are sold out in minutes. She is always in one of the stadiums because she commands such a large crowd. I don't know how well she knew Jane, but I do remember she was the guest of Jane's husband, Pastor Ron, a couple of years ago. I am not sure if she established a relationship with Jane and they kept in touch; I don't know. She doesn't seem to be Jane's type because Jane was very low-key, and this woman is the total opposite.

But, as I think about this, she could have been a friend of Jane's because Jane was the type of person that everybody loved because she made everyone feel so welcomed. You never had to put on airs with Jane, so perhaps she was the type of friend where Elona was able to let her hair down and be herself. I must remember to ask her about Plessey Humphrey; Jane mentioned in her letter that Plessey, a friend of Elona might need help.

I remember another pastor and wife who were sitting at the family table during the dinner, after the visit to the gravesite that I did not know. I remember introducing myself to them, Patricia and Gregory Harris. I was unsure of their connection to Jane and Ron. They were a young African American couple, and they appeared very close to Ron and the family. Patricia was very sad and didn't say very much to anyone. It seemed as if the family was consoling her as much as they were consoling each other. It appeared to be a very close connection.

There were so many people at this funeral, but these ladies really stuck out in the crowd. They were graceful and well dressed.

As a white Presbyterian pastor's wife, I began to wonder how in the world I could even get close to these first ladies. We ran in totally different circles, and I never saw them. I had to find some way to connect with three African American first ladies and an English evangelist from London. As a favor to my friend, I must reach out to these ladies.

I was beginning to feel overwhelmed. I had nothing but Jane in common with these people and, as of the funeral, that commonality had been lost. I have visited Pastor Terri's church, and I am familiar with their ministry, but the pastor and his wife were strangers to me. Even with their large ministry in Miami Beach, I don't know anything personally about them.

Everyone knows Elona Braggs because she is an international evangelist from London who comes to the United States often for ministry, but once Elona left the States, how would I reach her? I don't know her well enough to have any of her numbers.

Jane seemed to care about everybody but herself. One might even say she didn't care enough about herself. How she died doesn't say much about her closest friends. We talked every day, but she never shared anything with me that would give me the impression she was suicidal.

I have had many requests in my lifetime, but never anything like this. I have counseled people pro bono to help a friend, but I have never been given such a monumental task.

It is clear that Jane must have been hurting deeply and would have a pretty good idea of what was going on with her friends. I took this request seriously because Jane took her life. If she believed her friends might be any place near where she was, I understood the request and her concern.

As I think about these ladies, whatever they were feeling or whatever their situation might be, it is not apparent from the outside. They don't appear to be crying out for help. Could it be a silent cry?

CHAPTER 3

Tomorrow Is Another Day

God what am I to Do

I sat in the back of St. Marks Ministries, the African-American megachurch, home to Pastor Terri and Larry Jones, observing the First Lady's every move.

The church, located in South Florida, was an impressive building with bright colors and flags hanging everywhere. I wasn't sure what the flags all meant, but they looked great. Although they were not far from the ocean, there was this huge manmade lake right outside of the church. Two sides of the church were mostly glass so you could look out and see the water. It was a gorgeous view.

I didn't tell anyone I was going; I just wanted to make this first visit after Jane's death anonymous. I wore a hat, which was in order, as most of the ladies in attendance had on hats. I kept my shades on because I didn't want anyone to notice me. I was on BCN recently, talking about the suicide and other similar problems we have in megachurches. I talked about the pressure that comes with being a leader of a major ministry, not just megachurches, because we have found there is a great deal of pressure in all churches, especially when there are financial constraints. I had been pretty busy commentating on all sorts of issues surrounding suicide and depression and giving advice on how to detect this kind of problem early on with high-profile people, including businesswomen in high-profile jobs as well. So it was important to me that nobody recognized me at the church.

It was a great service; I would guess around 3,500 people were in attendance. They appeared to be from all walks of life; it was a great mix. Though it was a predominately African-American church, there were quite a few Hispanics and Cubans there as well. The pastor spoke in both English and Spanish; now that was something to see.

Coming from a Presbyterian church where we don't have a lot of moving around, this church made you want to dance. It was a dancing, shouting church, where everybody seemed to be enjoying themselves, including me. What a great worship service. It was a little long for me, but overall it was great. One thing that I loved about the church was that the offering was taken up when you first walked through the doors, so there was no time set aside for offering during the service. When the preacher finished preaching, an altar call was made, and after all the announcements had been given, you were dismissed. That is very similar to how we handle our offering, I just thought it was unusual for this type of church, but I loved it. I loved it because the service seemed to move faster. I went to observe the First Lady, and that's exactly what I did. She was an integral part of the service. She didn't walk in with the pastor; she came in about 10 minutes after he walked in, and when she did, the minister in charge announced her arrival and the church went up in excitement. Her smile brightened up the room. It was obvious the members were in love with their First Lady.

There is something about the first lady that brings things together; especially the first lady who understands one of the most important things is to love the people. It was obvious this was Pastor Terri. From my experience, not as a psychologist but as a First Lady of my church, I just loved on the people. No matter what's going on, I make sure they know their First Lady loves them, and that they are important to the First Family.

Pastor Terri walked in, so graceful and elegant. She was immaculately dressed with a small yet stunning hat. Her dress was mint green with a touch of pink. Her hat was a mint green that matched her dress perfectly. She was a tall lady with smooth, flawless brown skin and long wavy hair. When she sat down, the pulpit took on a totally different aura. Her presence was so magnetic it seemed as if everyone had their eyes on her when she entered the room.

As I watched Pastor Terri after the service, despite all her elegance, she seemed so approachable and personable; members were running up to the stage, and she was hugging them all. As I moved to the front of the stage, I wasn't sure what I would say. As I caught Pastor Terri's eye, there was this warm smile that came over her face. It was clear she remembered me. She hugged me with tears in her eyes and said, "I was expecting you. I don't know why, but I was expecting you." *Oh my God.*

I thought about Jane's connection with these first ladies as we talked briefly, and I mentioned Jane. She smiled as if she knew Jane had talked to me. We scheduled lunch for the very next day. I left the church with such a great feeling. I knew Jane had wanted me to talk to these ladies, but I had no idea that the very first person I would talk to would be so inviting. I was so excited about this lunch. Terri seemed to want to talk to me as well.

On my drive home, I couldn't stop thinking about the service and how wonderful it was. It was amazing how much Pastor Terri seemed to add to the service. It certainly was a great service, but when she walked into the room, it seemed to get even better.

I began to go over in my mind the conversation I would have with Pastor Terri. Why did she seem so eager to talk with me? What did she want to share with me? I thought about just having a nice lunch for our first visit; I would just get to know her, and we would make small talk. I thought about talking about her husband and the church, and I knew she had small children, so we would talk about what the children were doing. We would talk about her role in the ministry; I knew she was full-time, and that would be a great way to break the ice. I would talk about my church and my husband's ministry. I am not full-time in the ministry because of my practice, but I keep really busy.

Members don't think about you being part-time; as far as they are concerned, you are the first lady, with all the responsibilities that come with the title. It's important to me as a first lady that I never make excuses because I have other outside activities. I must always take the time to give attention to our members. Sometimes, people feel the first lady's place is a glamorous position; that all the first lady does is dress up and smile. The truth is–this is ministry at the highest level. Your service is not only to your husband; holding him up, encouraging him and protecting him, but also to your members and supporting the ministry.

We could spend hours talking about this kind of stuff. I turned into my driveway, feeling really good about this first meeting. I had figured everything out on the drive home. However, once I pulled my car in the driveway, doubt began to set in; I began to think about this first visit. "What if it didn't go this way? What if there was a turn toward some real serious conversation?" Well, I would deal with that if it came up.

I got so excited about the idea of talking with her about her life and our lunch that I didn't think about our friend Jane. I knew that would be a part of our conversation. I couldn't begin to know how to bring Jane up in conversation, and I had no idea where our conversation would go from there. Would I have the courage to tell her that right before Jane took her life; she wanted me to talk to some of her friends that she knew were in trouble? I knew I was going to need God's direction on this.

When I got out of my car, I walked into the house and my husband, Jonathan, greeted me. He could see I was drained and opened his arms, and I sort of collapsed in his arms. He'd known where I was going, but I didn't go into detail as to why I was going. I had gone to our service that morning, which started at 8 am, so I was pretty worn out. Jonathan and I tell each other everything; we really don't have any secrets. I knew I had to come up with the right time to share Jane's letter. He was so supportive with everything I did, particularly my work, but I think he knew this was more than work. Yes, it was work, but it was also ministry.

I was on assignment, and I knew it. I had never been so sure of anything in all my life. My practice as a psychologist has always been a professional undertaking for me. Although I am a pastor's wife, I never thought of it as a ministry. I have counseled many people, those with deep depression, those with mental challenges, but I never thought of it as part of my ministry. My ministry was at church, working with my husband, not in my office, but this calling to ministry hit me like a ton of bricks. I thought back on something I forgot Jane shared with me many years go; that all I do is ministry. What Jane was trying to tell me was to help her friends. She said, "If anybody can help them, you can."

I realized what Jane was talking about. I felt so privileged to have known Jane; I realized this was an awesome responsibility that I had been given, one that I didn't take lightly.

I always had the answers how I served my business clients. I now realized they were part of my ministry as well.

I was at a loss for words. I must handle these women of God like I should have been handling all of my clients: as part of my ministry.

These women have a calling on their lives, and whatever personal issues they may have, they have a higher calling that must be recognized, acknowledged, and considered in any decisions they make. I didn't know if I was worthy of looking into these ladies' hearts and minds. I just knew that I was on assignment, and God was directing me. I believed He would give me the strength and the words to say that may even save a life.

It was Monday morning, and I woke up early. I thought I would walk down to my study and make a few notes because today was the day Pastor Terri Jones and I would be meeting for lunch. Before I did anything, I prayed, "Lord, guide my footsteps, give me the words you want me to say, I am on assignment for you."

I was meeting Pastor Terri at a wonderful cafe on the water in Miami Beach. I had been there several times before as had Pastor Terri; it was a pretty popular place, a bit expensive, but the ambiance was worth it. We were scheduled to meet at noon on Monday. We had reservations, and I had requested this great corner table that was somewhat secluded from most of the other patrons with a fantastic view. I got there a little early, around 11:45; because I wanted to make sure we got the right table.

When I walked in and gave them my name, the young lady said, "Your party is already here." I was shocked, I turned the corner, and there was Pastor Terri sitting in one of the seats I'd reserved. She was simply stunning. She had on a beautiful white linen jumpsuit; I had never seen anything like that before. We hugged each other, and she seemed very glad to see me. When we sat down, neither one of us spoke; it was just quiet. She looked at me, her shoulders seemed to droop, and she said, "I miss Jane."

At that point, both of us began to shed tears. She began to talk about how she and Jane met at a pastors' conference. Jane's husband was one of the speakers, and the First Ladies had sat together and became fast friends. They had been friends for the last twenty years. She explained that they'd shared a lot of common experiences.

By that time, the waitress came over to the table and asked if we were ready to order. We both said we needed more time and gave our menus our undivided attention for the next few minutes so that when the waitress came back around, we were ready. This place had great seafood, so we both ordered one of the restaurant's specialties. While waiting for our meals, we made small talk about her children and their schools. Once the food came, we talked a little about how traumatic Jane's death was because everyone who met her loved her and she had seemed so happy. I then looked seriously at Terri, and asked her, "Well, how are you doing? Are you okay?"

She looked at me and dropped her head. When she raised it again, her eyes were filled with tears, but there was complete silence. She appeared to be crying inside. I didn't know what to do or say. The expression on her face was as if she was trying to communicate with me soundlessly. I asked her if there was anything I could do, and she said with a very quiet voice, "there is nothing anybody can do for me." I asked her if her health was okay and she said she was fine. "What about your husband and the children?"

She said they were all okay. I knew it wasn't financial, but I asked, "Is it money problems?"

She smiled and said no.

I looked at her and whispered, "Is it another woman?"

She shook her head and said no.

I didn't know what else to say. I then told her I didn't want to guess and asked her if she wanted to share it with me and she said yes, but seemed very hesitant. So I decided not to push her, and I changed the subject. I asked her if they were attending the pastors' conference in Dallas this year, and she said she wasn't sure. I told her my husband was presenting so we would be there. I continued to talk about the conference, the topics, and the other presenters.

Abruptly she said, "My husband beats me."

I said, "Excuse me?"

She said, "My husband physically hits me on a regular basis. I have been living with this for the last ten years."

I couldn't say a word; I was so shocked. She began to cry very quietly and so did I. Oh my God; never did I expect this in a million years. I remembered Jane saying this may be an issue. It's not that I had not heard this before; people had shared horrendous experiences with me. This poised, beautiful woman who seemed to have everything under control shocked me. She appeared to have a loving family and a beautiful church family who seemed to adore her. I said in a very quiet voice, "Do you want to talk about it?"

Still crying, with tears now running down her cheeks, she said, "There is nothing to talk about."

I said, "of course, there is something to talk about. I am sure I can help you." My training and contacts in the city afforded me a wealth of knowledge when it came to support services. I told her again, "I could help, let me help."

Terri wiped her eyes and said she appreciated the offer, but she was sure there was nothing I could do. I persisted because I knew I could help her. She finally said to me, "Mary, I am forty-six years old. I have two children, one in grade school and one in junior high school, who have lived a very good life and have become accustomed to their living arrangements.

We live in a gated community in an affluent neighborhood and they are both in private schools. I have never worked; I never went to school after high school. I wanted to, but my husband said he needed me by his side as he built this ministry. I have no skills. I have two secretaries, one who drafts my letters and helps me with any messages, and another who handles my schedule and the children's schedules. I cook some, but not very much; we have help in the house.

I wanted to leave ten years ago, but I didn't have any place to go. My family would not understand. I wouldn't dare tell my mother; it would break her heart.

I thought about Jane, how free she is today; she doesn't have to worry about her problems anymore. I seriously considered what Jane did. I thought about it ten years ago. After Jane actually did it, I felt maybe I could do it too, but I thought about my fourteen-year-old daughter. I just couldn't do that to her. I just couldn't. I would rather suffer than have her suffer the loss of me."

I said, "Terri, I really can help you," but Terri quickly interrupted. She said, "Mary, all you can do is put me in a shelter, and I can't do that. I have a responsibility not only to my immediate family, but also to my church family. I counsel women about this very thing. What would it look like if I moved out to a shelter? The hope and confidence that I have given to so many women would be shattered. I have no right to do that to them. I can't do that to them, and I will not do that to them." She said with determination etched in her voice.

Our food had been sitting on the table for about 30 minutes, and even if they warmed it up, I couldn't have eaten a thing. I asked Terri if she wanted me to have them warm the food up, and she said no, but that she would take a hot cup of coffee. I ordered two.

Terri began asking me questions about the pastors' conference in Dallas, when I was going, and explained that they had gone every year. She really wanted to go, and said she would ask her husband about their plans. She just started talking about the conference and other church matters as if she hadn't just confessed to being abused; she went into first lady mode. I followed her lead.

We drank our coffee and had a few more pleasantries and then walked together toward our cars. I told Terri I really wanted to stay in touch and talk some more, she said that would be great as if nothing traumatic or earth shattering ever transpired.

I got in my car and sat there for at least 30 minutes, staring out the window, until I said aloud, "GOD WHAT AM I TO DO."

I could feel myself holding back tears and felt so overwhelmed by the weight that I almost couldn't breathe, and I cried out again, "GOD WHAT AM I TO DO," and about that time, I couldn't control the tears, it was as if the burden she was carrying had become my burden. I looked around the parking lot trying to figure out which way was home, and I drew a blank. I am a well-trained certified psychologist with three degrees, and I have counseled hundreds of people with similar problems, but this was different, I asked God why it was different, and He said to me: *She is at the end of her rope, and you are ALL SHE'S GOT.*

With that, I started driving and found my way home. When I got home, I parked the car in the garage and went into the house. My husband greeted me in the hall, on his way from the living room. I smiled as best as I could and said, "I am really tired."

My husband said, "It must have been one of those days." I looked at him and said, "Yes it's been one of those days."

When I reached the edge of my bed, I knelt down to pray. All I could say was "God Help Me" and I went to bed. I didn't dream, I laid down and nothing came to my mind, I didn't think about Terri or her dilemma, I just went into a sound sleep with my spirit quietly whispering, "Tomorrow is another day."

CHAPTER 4

They Were All Living A Lie

Living behind the Mask

$\mathcal{S}$everal days, weeks, and then months passed and I didn't call or hear from Pastor Terri. I was very concerned because I remembered what God said to me, and I knew something needed to happen soon. I continued to pray for her and ask God for direction.

One evening, I got home from work, and my husband said, "In about three weeks on a Saturday, we are going to see an old friend of Jane's."

I asked him who, and he replied, "Elona Braggs, the English evangelist who attended Jane's funeral."

"Where did you get the tickets?" I asked. "Her events are normally sold out before she gets here, like months in advance."

My husband said, "It was the strangest thing. Elona Braggs remembered us and personally had someone drop them by the church. She said she would like to see us after the service. We have backstage passes as well."

I was literally shaking. My husband didn't see me, but I asked God if this was a sign. After my experience with Pastor Terri, I was really too afraid to even make contact with the rest of the ladies. I needed some time.

Elona Braggs was a very charismatic person. But, if you watched her when she was away from the crowd, and away from her followers, she seemed very egotistical and not very friendly. You would never think that if you met her. I wondered why she would give tickets to my husband, and want to see us after the service. Although, I was sure she remembered us from a few intimate dinners at Jane's home, we didn't know her well.

The meeting would be held in three weeks, and my main concern was if this would be a good time to talk with her, and if not, when would be a better time? I knew our conversation must be in person. But it seemed impossible to imagine a time that would be right as she moved so quickly whenever she was in the States, going from one meeting to the next, and then off to London. I wondered if I should contact her before the meeting and try to meet with her in private so there would not be a lot of distractions. I didn't know what to do, but I decided I was going to attempt to make contact the next day. She did write a number on the tickets; I assumed it was her personal number and decided to see what would happen.

I was never given any directions on how to carry out these contacts with Jane's friends. I prayed about it and asked for direction, but God had not given me any clarity. All I knew was that I was to contact each one of them.

The task had become a tremendous undertaking. I wanted to do it, but at the same time, I felt I needed to get on with my life. No one would know anything about Jane's request but me; I never really shared Jane's wish with anyone. I guess I knew the day might come when I would just try to walk away, quietly, but I knew I couldn't do that; I knew this was a Divine request from God. Jane may have requested it, but God had His hands in this and I was not going to disobey him. I knew he knew my mandate and I needed to find the courage and the strength to push forward and do all I could to reach these women.

"Tomorrow is another day," I thought. "God, give me strength and the wisdom to do what I know is your will, and give me what you would have me say. I don't want my ego to get mixed up in this; I need this to be all you."

Elona usually got into town for one of her services two days before it started, so I had some time to figure out when I would try to see her. I knew I probably should wait until after her crusade, but I decided to contact her office and make an appointment to see her, if possible, before the crusade.

It was summertime, and the flowers painted the landscape with their vibrant colors. The weather was great. It doesn't rain a lot in Miami this time of the year, and it was really hot, but down by the ocean, early in the morning, you get a cool breeze; I would often go over to Miami Beach and walk along the seashore just to talk with God, and hopefully get some answers from him. That summer morning, I was driving to Miami Beach. I hadn't done this for a while — not since I visited Pastor Terri's church. I got up and just decided to go. I work out pretty often, leaving for the gym early in the morning. It was not unusual for my husband to see me off to the gym, so it didn't occur to my husband to ask where I was going. I didn't say I wasn't going to the gym; I just got up with my mind set on driving to Miami Beach and that's what I did.

I drove there to receive from God how I was to handle Elona Braggs. As soon as I got out of my car, the only person I could think about was Pastor Terri. I was concerned with how she was doing and feeling very guilty because I had not called her. After getting out of my car, I gave Pastor Terri a call. She answered the phone. I apologized for calling so early, and told her I had come over to Miami Beach to walk along the seashore and pray.

She quickly said, "May I join you?"

I said, "Of course."

She replied, "Now, tell me, exactly where you are?"

I explained, "Right behind the Miami Beach and Spa hotel, standing next to the outdoor café."

She knew exactly where I was and said she was on her way.

Wow! I hadn't expected her to react this way; it was as if she wanted to see me. While I was waiting, I decided to stop by the outdoor café that was open early for breakfast, for people like me who might want an energy drink or just a great cup of coffee. I had a cup of coffee and a bagel while I waited for Pastor Terri. There was a cool breeze by the ocean, and the sky was bright blue without a cloud in the sky. The sand and water seemed to stretch to eternity. It was the most perfect day.

I asked God while I sat and waited to guide me, to give me what to say. I didn't want to be judgmental. I knew I was shocked, but I began to realize that I was also angry the last time I saw Terri; I couldn't believe she would let him beat her. I just couldn't believe that. I thought she was coming to tell me that it wasn't true. Maybe she just wanted to get my attention, but she didn't know how to do it; maybe she was hurting for other reasons and wanted me to definitely take notice of her. I don't know; I just don't know, but she certainly got my attention. As all of this was going through my mind, I looked up and there was this stunning woman walking toward me in a grey and blue workout suit and a blue and grey Dallas Cowboys cap on her head, with these fabulous designer glasses covering half of her face.

Pastor Terri looked great. We were both glad to see each other. We hugged as if we were long-lost friends. I wanted to apologize for not getting back to her. She said she missed talking with me, and we both said we missed talking with Jane, and then we both began to cry.

I explained to Pastor Terri that I came to Miami Beach to seek God's wisdom regarding Evangelist Elona Braggs, and Terri knew of her, but not personally. She just knew Elona was a great evangelist and had met her once through Jane. I explained to Terri that Elona was another person Jane had asked me to talk with, and I needed to seek God's wisdom as to how to approach her. Pastor Terri began to express how difficult she thought that would be since Elona lived in London and she was only here for her crusades, but she said; "God will find a way for you."

"Enough about her, how are you doing, Terri?" I replied. "Have things changed, or are they about the same?"

"Things are somewhat better," Terri said. "I discovered the best way to refrain from confrontation was to stay out of my husband's way. Make myself invisible, literally tiptoeing around on the tile floors. He took his first vacation alone without the family. He went to Europe, and he said he needed to get away on a regular basis, alone. Of course, I agreed with him and said it may help things at home. He began working late and was coming to bed late and then he just stopped coming into the bedroom at all to sleep. He only comes in to get dressed. I dared not say anything. This has been going on for the last two months."

I asked Pastor Terri, "Is there anything I can do to help?"

She said she didn't think so. She felt her children had a great life; they had everything they ever thought they wanted. I wanted to tell Pastor Terri, the children she thinks are happy see everything going on in that house and, if things were as she said; their life is not all that great. What children want is love in a home; that's what makes them happy. Pastor Terri had described a very unhappy place where vacations are being taken alone, and her husband was now sleeping someplace else in the house. Why is it we think our world is so great when there is no love in the home, when the only things cherished are clothes, big houses, and big cars?

I asked Pastor Terri how the church was doing, and she said it was great. "It's growing by leaps and bounds," she said. She was working very hard in the church, and they put on a great front that their marriage was wonderful, and the children were happy in their big beautiful home. I wondered if the members had a clue about these separate vacations, and what they would think if they knew. I wondered if any of them knew how physically abusive Pastor Larry was to Pastor Terri. I wondered if they knew Pastor Terri and Pastor Larry hadn't slept together for months in this wonderful place they call home.

It was amazing how Pastor Terri's face lit up when she talked about ministry. It was very obvious that her church was the most important area of her life. I could really see that. I saw how the members had reacted to her when she walked into the church, on that Sunday morning. They really loved her. Some first ladies come to the realization, with experience and over time, that this was their assignment. God had placed them in this position and they must be accountable to him.

There were others who just couldn't handle the pressure, and they had taken a back seat to all that was going on because it was just too much to handle, along with what was going on at home. When a first lady adopts this attitude, the church is well aware that all is not well. I am reluctant to say, we have to do what must be done for the ministry and for the people, but where does this leave the first lady?

It was very obvious to me that Pastor Terri could continue to live as she was living the rest of her life. She had fabulous clothes. She'd adjusted to the fact that there would be private vacations without her or the children. Pastor Larry had chosen not to share their bed, and every now and then she had to be concerned with physical abuse. All of this seemed okay to her. I asked Pastor Terri if this was the life she wanted to live. She said, "No, but it's a life that's manageable."

She explained she saw so many struggling pastors and churches, but God had blessed her with a man who was anointed and blessed the people every Sunday. She explained she was able to help in meeting the needs of the people. With all that was going on in her personal life, the ministry and the people kept her going, and she believed in her heart this was her responsibility. She understood it came at a price but she was willing to make the sacrifice.

I didn't know what to say to that. At that point, I didn't know if I could help her, simply because she seemed content with where she was in her life. I didn't think she was content being in an abusive relationship, but she was content with the understanding that this was where she needed to be in the ministry. The people needed her, and she wanted to be there for them. My concern was, who was there for the First Lady?

I felt really bad for her because I don't think she realized what she was saying. In essence, she was saying she would rather be personally unhappy; this was the cross she must bear. How do you stand in a pulpit on Sunday preaching love, kindness, and forgiveness when you are living the opposite?

How many people do that? How many people are living a lie?

I told Pastor Terri that if she needed me, I was just a phone call away. It just seemed to me that how her life was structured, it was like a time bomb waiting to go off, and I was so afraid she might not be able to handle it.

I reflected on some of her conversations about Pastor Larry coming home late and sleeping someplace other than his bedroom in the house. It just sounded like there was someone else in this picture that might emerge and shatter Pastor Terri's comfortable and manageable lifestyle. Because of so many other things she had shared with me, I didn't think she would be able to handle this kind of confrontation. She was so concerned about never finishing school and not being able to take care of herself and her children. Pastor Terri felt she had no place to go, so she took the abuse, but what if she had a place to go?

Pastor Terri and I had been walking for about an hour.

I invited Pastor Larry and Terri to Christmas dinner well in advance of the holidays to make sure they put it on their calendar. I was hoping they would join me for the holidays to celebrate the life of Jane Steinbeck, a holiday dinner in her honor. She said they would definitely be there. She loved the idea.

Pastor Terri and I reached the breakfast cafe. We hugged each other. I told her I didn't want this much time to pass again before we got together, and she agreed. We got into separate cars, my Volvo wagon and her SUV Mercedes. As she drove off, I thought, *"Well it sure looks as if she has a great life, but looks are deceiving."*

Jane, my dear beloved Jane, had given me this mandate to help her friends. After getting to know Pastor Terri, it struck me like a load of bricks: Jane's friends were just like her. They were pretending that everything was great. They're acting as if their lives, their homes, their marriages, and their children were wonderful. The success was all around them—the big church, the large membership. The friends of Jane were just like her, they had made it, and they were at the top. Maybe all of them were not truly at the top, but they looked the part; if they were struggling, you never saw that side of them. I now realized this great dilemma. The people Jane asked me to work with were just like her; so how in the world would I pierce through this veil? How would I reach in there and pull them out?

This was a God-sized problem; I didn't have a clue how to help these women. I couldn't help my best friend? I couldn't pull her out? I had no idea she was hurting and giving up, all at the same time.

CHAPTER 5

The Crusade

Lonely but not Alone

As I continued to think through how I was going to reach these women who were hurting, so many things were going through my mind. Sometimes one thinks, *"If I had money, it would solve most of my problems."* Maybe it would solve many of my problems, but is it enough to keep me sane? Is that enough reason for me to get up in the morning? I thought about Jane.

One of the issues Pastor Terri shared with me was that it was so difficult on Sunday mornings to get motivated to go to church. That surprised me because these people loved her, but I think she felt she was living a lie. Encouraging people that they could make it, that all they needed was faith in God; well, she had faith in God, or did she? What happens when you get so involved, so up-close and personal in ministry where you clearly love the Lord and believe and have faith, but you lose sight of this wonderful truth, that you can do all things through Christ, who strengthens you.

What has caused this loss of enthusiasm? Was her faith gone? Was her love for the church gone because it was so difficult, Sunday after Sunday, to prepare for Church, put on her First lady face and greet the people? From what she shared with me that day on the beach this was how Pastor Terri felt. Sunday after Sunday it was getting harder and harder to dredge up the energy to go. She had money and the kind of luxury that many only dreamed about. I understood Pastor Terri a lot more than Jane, who took her own life.

Pastor Terri was dealing with a man who was abusive, and she was doing all she could to save her marriage. She believed she had to go through what she was going through for the sake of the children and herself. But what happened to Jane? I clearly knew her husband was not abusive to her; she had a great life and seemed to enjoy being in worship with the members. I just don't know. I wish I knew more. I understand my professional field is helping clients work through their issues, drawing the thoughts of loneliness, depression, and suicide out into the open.

If I could only convince them to believe what they preached and taught at their churches: God never fails. He will never leave us. He will bring comfort and reassurance that He can do abundantly more than we could ask or think. He is the savior of the world, and He can fix anything. A broken heart is not too hard for God. A broken home, He can repair, and a broken marriage, He can mend and make it brand new. When things get so hard to bear, and you find yourself crying, and you are really unsure why you're crying, God can wipe away the tears and put a smile on your face. He can brighten up your day, and when you think you can't make it, He's right there to say, YES YOU CAN.

I know I could help these young ladies. My God is an awesome God; he holds the solutions to each problem, each heartache. He had me on assignment, and He was going to give me what I needed for each one of them. What they were experiencing was just a foretaste of what God would do through them when they completely surrendered. They would be so powerful, so anointed, so on fire for God, if they just lived what they preached.

Elona Braggs' crusade was in a couple of days. I tried to reach her several times, but was unable to get hold of her, so I knew it was meant for us to talk when I saw her after the crusade.

Elona would be ministering at the Miami Beach Convention Center. It was completely sold out. My husband and I had tickets to her meeting and separate backstage passes for after the meeting. She was extremely successful and always looked like she had everything together. What in the world could be going on in her life, where Jane felt she needed my help? In Jane's letter, she specifically mentioned these four women by name and said, please help. Elona was single, and I don't think she was ever married. I'd never heard in the news or the tabloids of her having a boyfriend or girlfriend. In fact, I'd only heard wonderful things about her and her ministry.

Elona Braggs was tall and beautiful, with blonde hair, piercing blue eyes and dimples. She must have been at least five foot eleven or six feet tall. She reminded me of a European model. She was known all over the world; I was not sure how Elona knew Jane, but they didn't appear to have anything in common. Elona was very cosmopolitan; she wore and carried designer everything. But after listening to her on several talk shows, I realized she was very different in spite of all of this popularity, fame, and success, she was a nice person and appeared to be very kind. She was easily entreated, humble and down-to-earth, very approachable. Now that I think about it, she had some of the same qualities as Jane. I could see them being friends; it was clear that both of them loved the Lord and had a passion for ministry. When Elona opened her mouth, you knew right away she was an anointed woman of God. She transformed into this powerful preacher. She wasn't an excitable preacher or a demonstrative preacher; she just stood flat-footed and preached the word of God. Her eyes were so piercing that when watching her on TV, she looked as if she was talking directly to you. She was a gifted prayer warrior. When she began to pray you wanted to keep your eyes open because her prayers were so powerful, you didn't want to miss anything. You didn't want to miss what she was saying, and you didn't want to miss seeing the anointing that engulfed her as she prayed. When she began to talk about God's grace and forgiveness, it made you want to find someone and ask them, "If there is anything I have done to you, please forgive me."

When she spoke, the presence of God was so thick in the room, the room seemed to fill up with smoke, but it was more like a thick fog. I wish I could really describe what it looked like. She was so powerful when she prayed. You felt blessed, inspired, and immediately uplifted if you were feeling down. There was a sense of hope that got down in your spirit, letting you know you could make it.

My husband was excited about being at the crusade. We were planning to go a couple of hours early. Although we had good seats, the parking was going to be very congested, and we wanted a good parking space.

We left early, and we were in our seats, the fifth row, front and center, almost an hour before the service was to begin. There were hundreds of people there when we arrived. The stadium seated about 20,000 people, and it was expected to be totally full.

Right before the crusade started, the stadium was so packed I didn't see an empty seat. A praise team came out first. This was a group in the U.S. that always sang at Elona's crusades. It was an African American group of five women; one was a harpist, who sounded like an angel from on high. They set the atmosphere. Although we were in a stadium, this was God's house, and they ushered the anointing in with the song "Anointing Fall on Me." It was divine. I looked around. Everyone seemed to be on one accord, with hands lifted up, crying out to God. By the time Evangelist Braggs came out, people were so ready to receive the word of God; she didn't have to say much. She briefly gave some pleasantries and then went right to the word. She used the topic "Mirror, Mirror, on the Wall, Can You See Jesus in Me at All." It was a powerful message.

After her message, she thanked everyone for coming and thanked them for their sacrifice. Because the tickets were fifty dollars, she said she was not taking up an offering; the purchase of the ticket was more than enough to bless her ministry.

Then, she said something quite interesting. She said, "If you feel a need to give, there will be forty people who are stretched across the front of the stage on the floor with receptacles to accept those gifts." She said again, "I am not taking up an offering, you have already blessed my ministry by buying a ticket, but if you are led to give and have a need to give, whatever amount you choose, start coming now."

"Oh my God," I said, as I saw the people move. It was a stampede. You would have thought she'd said, "I am giving one hundred dollar bills away; first come, first serve." People started coming from every aisle, every row, those in the balcony, they were coming. People were standing in line to get

close to the baskets. I had never seen anything like that. She didn't say she would pray for them, she didn't say she would lay hands on those that gave. She just said she would allow the people to give.

We gave because God blessed us through the word, and we felt the need to give. My husband jumped up and said, "I am giving a hundred for you and a hundred for me," and that pleased me very much because we were on one accord. By the time he got back to his seat, she was giving a benediction, and people were still in the aisles waiting to give. After she dismissed us, the people in the aisles waited patiently to give. Nobody got out of the line; they wanted to give, they felt a need to give. We stayed in our seats because we knew we were supposed to go backstage to see Elona. There were so many people in the aisles that we just decided to be patient. Elona had already left the stage. She had to be completely worn out. She had ministered for at least two hours.

Her praise team was singing beautiful worship songs as the people were giving. The harpist with a portable harp began walking through the aisles, the sound was simply amazing. We enjoyed sitting and listening to them worship and watching the people continue to praise the Lord.

Finally, the crowd died down, and we were able to make our way to the back of the stage. We showed our backstage passes, and they let us through. We just knew there would be this huge crowd, and we really were hoping to get to see and at least speak to Elona and shake her hand. I wanted to let her know who we were and explain that we were Jane's friends; hopefully, with that, she might spend a little time with us. We were directed to go to the south green room. The gentleman opened the door and nobody was in there, so we sat down, quite puzzled. Where was everybody? Since this was the south green room, was everybody in the north green room, and someone else would be coming to take us there? We couldn't figure it out. The gentleman who let us in said someone would come to get us, so we just waited patiently. Thirty minutes passed, and I just figured they'd forgotten us and Elona had gone back to her hotel. I told my husband we would wait for twenty more minutes, and then we were going to go. At about that time, a side door opened, not the one we came in but another door, and it was Elona Braggs, apologizing because she had to speak to some people in the north green room. I realized right then that we were the only people invited to the south green room.

"Are you ready?" Elona asked.

I said, "Well, yes," but I didn't have a clue what she was talking about. She said we were going over to her condo and someone would bring us back to our car. My mouth dropped wide open. We gathered up our things, followed her into another room and to a door that led outside; and there with its doors wide open was a stretched limousine. I said to myself, "Oh my God."

We got in and she apologized because her condo was about twenty minutes away from the convention center. She explained she had purchased a condo five years ago in Miami since she spent so much time in Florida. Elona asked us how we had been. When she mentioned that the last time she saw us was at Jane's funeral we began to talk about the funeral and how it was such a tragedy. She began staring into space and said, "I really miss Jane. She was a close friend and someone I talked to often."

I thought to myself, *"Jane never mentioned her friendship with Elona to me, and I talked to her almost every day."*

What I thought was quiet interesting was that Elona talked to us as if she knew us.

"Jane talked about you all the time; and I am really looking forward to getting to know you better," she said.

I told her we really were looking forward to getting to know her as well.

She asked, "Did Jane ever talk to you about me?"

I said, "Yes, she did." I didn't share with her that the only time she mentioned Elona was in her suicide note.

Elona said, "I know she didn't speak often about me. That's Jane, always keeping secrets."

I thought that statement was quite interesting because Jane never appeared to be one that kept secrets. But I could never be more wrong. I really missed it; she must have kept many secrets. She took her life, and I never knew anything was wrong. I would say she not only kept secrets, but big secrets, major secrets, life-threatening secrets, life-shattering secrets.

We arrived at the condo sooner than I expected. It was a really nice high-rise condominium. We were the only ones in the limo, and to our surprise, we were the only people at the condo other than those that were there to prepare and serve the meal. Elona was so friendly. She asked us about the crusade and how we liked it, and I told her, "It was an amazing service."

She was very pleased with the crusade. She was surprised it was sold out. I thought that was the norm, and I said as much.

She said, "They are, but I am always surprised at the turnout."

My husband asked her about London and her activities there. She explained she traveled so much; she didn't have much of a ministry in London. She did reveal she supported her brother's church; he had one of the oldest Presbyterian churches in London. It was very well established and through her brother's church she supported two orphanages in Africa and one in India. She said that was how she met Jane—in Johannesburg, at one of the orphanages dedication ceremony. Jane's church supported several schools in Africa.

Elona and the Steinbecks had been friends ever since the dedication. She said they ended up having dinner together in Johannesburg, and saw each other several times before they left. Jane and Elona continued to keep in touch once Jane got back to the States. Elona said they grew close and had been friends for over 20 years. "She was my confidant," Elona said, describing Jane as her rock. She began to look out into space and said, "I don't know how I am going to make it without Jane."

We talked about everything. I quickly confessed that Jane and I were also close. Elona asked me at that point what I did. I told her I was a psychologist and co-pastor of a Presbyterian church. Elona said, "Wow, you keep pretty busy," and I said, "Yes, I really do."

Elona had a great dinner prepared for us, and we had a wonderful fellowship. My husband shared some information regarding some of his work over in India with some of the villages and she seemed very interested.

In all, we had a great time. It was as if we had known each other for a very long time. We talked a lot about Jane, the shock we had over the loss of her, and how we were going to miss her. Neither of us had a clue about why Jane took her life. We both agreed she was such a support to everyone who knew her. To everyone, she was the strong one with comforting words and the anointed and powerful prayers. By the time we compared a few stories, we both were in tears. We embraced one another and Elona said, "I really need to keep in touch with you." She didn't just say she wanted to keep in touch with me; she said that she really needed to stay in touch with me. I thought, *"God, you have opened this door."* I didn't know how it was going to be opened, but I knew it had to be a God thing.

When we left Elona's condo, riding in her limo, my husband and I looked at each other speechless. We knew it was a divine connection. My husband said, "This was a divine connection. I don't know why, but it is."

I still had not told my husband anything about the letter Jane had left. I know that sounds crazy, but I had felt protective of this confidential information and maybe even slightly possessive of this assignment I was given. Right at that moment,

I knew it was time to share it with him. "Honey, I have something I have got to tell you."

He turned toward me. I said, "Better yet…"

I reached into my purse and pulled out the letter. I always carried it with me; I don't know why. I gave it to him and ask him to read it. He began to read it, but first he looked on the last page at the bottom to see who wrote the letter. He paused, looked at me and kept reading. At the end of the letter, there was silence, and then he turned to me and said, "Why didn't you tell me?"

I said, "I don't know, but I knew this was the time to share it with you."

I started crying profusely. "I am so glad you know; this has been such a heavy burden on me, and it is such a relief that somebody else knows."

He looked at me and just hugged me so tight as if to say, "It's all right now, we are in this thing together."

By the time I regained some of my composure, we were back at our car. As we exited the limo and got into our car, my husband didn't say a word—neither did I. I knew it was a lot to digest, and I began to think about Elona and when we would meet again. It seemed as if I had made more headway with her than Pastor Terri.

When my husband and I got home and into bed, he looked at me and said, "You should have told me. Why would you carry something like this by yourself?"

I explained, "I just went into work mode, and looked at this as a client sharing with me. I know she's dead, but it was difficult to say anything because I knew once I began talking with these women, my conversations would be confidential, but I was led to share the letter.

After you said this was a divine connection, I knew, at a minimum, you needed to understand the type of assignment I was on. And, well, I really needed your support."

He understood, he had always been supportive of my work, but he said this gave him what he needed so he could bombard Heaven for me. I was so relieved; it was as if a tremendous weight had been lifted off my shoulders. My shoulders had begun to hurt from all of the stress, but after speaking with my husband they finally felt light. I thanked God for my husband.

Two weeks later, I received a call from Elona Braggs; I was quite surprised. Although I knew we'd talked about getting together, I had no idea she would call me so soon. Two weeks was really not a long time for someone who had a busy schedule like Elona. She said she would be in town in about a week and thought it might be good if we could sit down and talk. I told her that would be great. I asked her where she wanted to meet, if she would like to schedule lunch or dinner. She said she wanted to schedule an appointment at my office.

I got quiet. She quickly said, "Mary, I need some of your professional help. I will certainly pay you for your time."

I knew Elona could pay me and wouldn't think anything of it, but I knew this was part of my assignment, and I couldn't take any money, so I said, "Don't worry about the money. When can you come in?"

She answered, "As soon as you can see me."

She had a scheduled crusade for March 15, and she would be in town a week before the crusade and two weeks after. She said any day but the 15th; whatever I had available was when she wanted to see me. I said, "How about the second day you're scheduled to be here?" I also said that if we could meet again before she left, that would be great.

So the appointment was scheduled for the 10th of March, for two hours from 2 p.m. to 4 p.m.

I told Elona I wanted to email her an intake sheet that was completed by everyone I saw; I wanted her to do that in advance so we wouldn't waste any time. She said that would be fine.

March 10th came so quickly. Elona was very prompt, and she was at my office at 1:45. She came alone; I was very surprised. I discovered she did have a driver who was downstairs waiting. I had received the intake form the same day I sent it to her.

I asked her where she wanted to sit. I had a very comfortable Queen Anne chair, a nice lounge chair that sat up halfway, and a very relaxing couch. She preferred the Queen Anne chair.

I told Elona, "Since this is our first consultation, I want you to talk about whatever you want to talk about." When it seemed she didn't know where to begin, I started by asking if she was ready for her crusade in a few days and if she was continuing to enjoy ministering in the U.S. She said she loved to minister anywhere; it was the gift that God had given her. She stated, "ministering as a single woman is very lonely, and sometimes you can get into trouble."

Elona went on to say, "I have been doing this for the last twenty years by myself, and my concentration has been focused on ministry. I didn't have many friends; there were many people around me, but I understood they were not all my friends. I had acquaintances, people who loved my ministry, those looking for me to give them a word, those who just wanted to be in my presence for whatever reason. I had a few friends—those people who I knew loved me, and some from my childhood—people who just loved me and were proud of my accomplishments and were concerned about my wellbeing. Although Jane was not from my childhood, I have known her most of my life in ministry. I shared a lot with Jane. She knew of many of my shortcomings, but she cared about me, never judging me when I made a mistake."

"We have all made mistakes that we have had to live with," I said. I wanted to talk about her loneliness and how she was dealing with it.

Elona began to explain, "That's how I got into trouble. I have dealt with being alone during my entire ministry, and I have never married. Sure, I have dated, but my problem was, I was never too sure if those I dated actually cared for me. They might have been just excited about my ministry. I knew I had to marry someone similar to me, not necessarily in ministry, but someone accomplished in his field. Someone secure within himself. I am not interested in a man looking at my paycheck and his paycheck and putting them together. I am sorry, Mary, I am not looking for that."

"That's understandable," I said, "But what about marrying someone for love in whatever state you find him in, recognizing you wouldn't be dating the person unless he met some of your criteria?"

Elona explained she was looking for love. "There are not that many men who fit in my category that are available. That's what got me into trouble."

Elona continued to explain, revealing a relationship involving a married man. She explained that she had done so well for fifteen years, rejecting all the married men who would approach her, and there were many. She also rejected the many female evangelists who approached her, and there were many.

Elona explained that in her younger days, she had to turn down many invitations because the pastors made it clear what was involved if she were allowed to minister in their church. She said, "There were so many young evangelists in their twenties who went along with it because they wanted to minister so badly, and they were trying to get their names out there. They did what they had to do; at least that's how they felt. Many have lived to regret it. The beauty of God's forgiveness is that it's unconditional and even though He knows our thoughts and our inclinations if we turn from our sins He forgives us.

This is how I have ministered to many of the young female evangelists. I told them to hold their heads up, God has forgiven them, and they must forgive themselves. But why can't I adhere to my own teachings? Why do I hurt so bad and feel so alone?"

I asked Elona if she was dating now, and she said she hadn't since she broke up with this married man, over a year ago. I asked why she wasn't dating now, and she said, "I guess I am still in love with him."

"Who broke off the relationship?" I asked.

She answered, "I did. I knew it was wrong. It was a relationship that had gone on for three years. I didn't want to start the relationship. I understood and knew my commitment toward my ministry and toward God. I was at one of the lowest points in my life; I was so lonely and he was a good friend who does what I do; he was an evangelist and did a lot of traveling. We were just friends. I was a friend to his wife and the children. They called me Aunt Lona. I felt just horrible. Although he was an evangelist, he was also a pastor. His wife, a first lady of a megachurch, was always poised, but I believed she knew he was seeing someone based on what she would say to me. We would be in a deep conversation, and she would always call him Pastor and say, 'One thing I know is that I have a responsibility and a commitment as first lady to my church. Pastor travels so much, it's important that I keep things going here.' She would say, 'This is my life, and these are God's people.'

"She was such a gracious woman and I felt so bad. I knew he would never leave her, and she would never leave him, and I didn't want them to leave each other. I just got caught up, and so did he. He said he loved me, and I know I loved him, but I knew that wasn't enough. When I ended the relationship, I explained I wanted this relationship to end with some dignity and respect for those who were around us and who have given so much meaning to our lives: his wife and children. By ending it with dignity, I asked that he not call me ever again and not make this any more difficult than it already was.

Whether she thought I was the woman involved with him or not, she never let on; she always hugged me when I saw her and requested when I come to the States to please come by because the children wanted to see me. That's the kind of woman she was. In some small way, I think she knew we had been involved, but at the same time she knew it was over.

So, Mary, that's my story, I have asked for forgiveness. Unfortunately, I continue to love this man, but we have not talked since the day we stopped seeing each other. He has called, but I have never responded to his phone calls. I wanted to go on with my life.

I would love to meet someone. As you know, my crusades are sold out when I come to the United States. There are so many people who approach me, so many breakfast and dinner engagements while I am here. I am quite busy but so lonely. It's hard to trust men, and as I have said before, there are just not that many out there that I would even consider."

I sat up in my chair, leaned over to Elona and looked her directly in her eyes.

In a soft voice I said, "The gift of ministering at the level you are ministering comes at a price; it's giving yourself away. As you know, Elona, Jesus said, 'If any man come after me, let him deny himself and take up his cross and follow me.'

Jesus invites us to embrace suffering in serving him. There is no getting around this. Be assured God's presence is always with you, even when you feel lonely. Be sensitive to the fact that God never leaves us alone; he places in our path people who understand and will affirm and encourage us. Be alert and sensitive to the Lord's provision to help you in your loneliness.

You must be open; don't build a wall of self-pity. You must be open to who God sends to help with your loneliness, and Elona, don't be so hung up with a man's financial standing. Be open. Don't miss out on your blessing."

Elona began to cry—this tall, stately woman who ministers to tens of thousands at a time began to cry. I put my arms around her and said, "We are going to take this one day at a time, and with time, it will get better. Elona, I want to see you again before you leave town. I want you to write down all of the qualities you would like to see in your husband, and I want you to prioritize those qualities based on the qualities that are most important to you. That will be our starting point when I see you in a few days. You help so many people through your ministry; that should give you great satisfaction."

Elona explained that the best part of her life was when souls were saved, when people had been closed to the gospel, and their eyes were opened. "My ministry is my life. If I could not minister, I would probably end up like Jane. I enjoy teaching and leading others to Christ. I am on such a high when ministering and right afterwards when sharing with those who come backstage, but when I come down, and everybody is gone, and I mean everybody, everything seems to change.

People think I have an entourage that travels with me. I have a musician and a secretary. There are a lot of people around, but they are not actually with me. It looks like they are, but only two people come from London, and they leave directly after my crusade, heading back to the hotel. I do contract a security team while I am in the States. They pretty much keep their distance. They make sure I get to the hotel or my condo, wherever I am staying, and they leave. I don't have very much conversation with the security personnel or the personnel who are responsible for bringing me to the States. I appear very aloof, but I have always been like that when traveling. I never want anything I say to be misunderstood, so I pretty much keep my distance. I certainly spend a lot of time with those who I minister to, but that's different.

When I retire to a hotel room; nobody is with me, just me. I get lonely, but I like being alone. Does that make any sense, Mary?"

"Of course it makes sense."

"Mary, I will be open. When I make my list of priorities, I can assure you at the top of my list is not a man with financial means to take care of me. Of course, that will be in there somewhere, but not at the top of my list. Thank you, Mary, for listening to me and being open."

CHAPTER 6

The Consult

Start from the Beginning

As we promised each other, Pastor Terri and I kept in touch. We would talk occasionally, most of it being light conversation. I was truly concerned about her and her home situation, but I knew if I continued to push and question her on it she might pull back. Imagine my surprise when one day, in the middle of a lighthearted chat, she asked if she could come in for a consultation. I kept my voice calm even though I wanted to shout "Thank You God."

I walked in my home office and pulled my schedule to make an appointment with her right away. As I thought over my preparation for Pastor Terri, I knew I was going to have to be very careful in our counseling sessions. She had openly and directly said to me that her husband, Pastor Larry Jones, was physically abusing her on a regular basis. My first discussion with Pastor Terri would have to start with whether she'd sought domestic violence support. She needed a group of professionals that were knowledgeable in this area. I also wondered if she had a place to keep the family safe while going through this period of transition.

I knew Pastor Terri was part of the Body of Christ and so was I. Although I am a Presbyterian, we believed in the same holy word of God, so in my counseling with Terri, I believed both of us would agree that abuse was completely opposite from God's nature and when you are a part of Him, you are completely a new creature.

I was not sure whether Pastor Terri had tried to talk with Pastor Larry about what was going on in the home, but if that had not worked, I thought it would be helpful if a professional such as myself and one of his spiritual leaders that was part of his denomination – someone he looked up to and respected – met with him and talked through what was going on at home. Clearly, there needed to be some type of intervention. If nothing else, I thought it was imperative that Pastor Terri consult with a domestic violence support group during this same time. She needed someone to help her decide whether it would be safe enough to stay in the home and the best people to do that would be the professionals who worked in that area on a daily basis. I recognized how Pastor Terri felt about talking with these types of counselors, but what do you say to someone you know is going through an abusive relationship? I felt I had no choice but to continue to talk to her about getting the help we both knew she needed. Although this abuse had continued off and on for ten years, I still had a responsibility once she shared with me to make sure the environment was safe for her and the children.

We, as a part of the Body of Christ, can't just sit and know what's happening and do nothing. What if something happened to the First Lady and you knew what was going on? You would never forgive yourself. Sometimes we have to reach out to someone else in authority, whether it's inside your denomination or someone outside that all parties respect and look up to. We cannot sit around and talk about it to our friends; as a friend, this is a responsibility we have to those we love.

I was never given the chance to help Jane. I would have talked with Jane, and if I knew she was so far gone, I would have made some calls and found her help. This is what friends do for one another.

I was scheduled to meet Pastor Terri in my office the next day. We had a two-hour consultation. My initial consultation was always two hours, and after the first meeting, our consultations would be one hour.

Terri walked into my office at the scheduled time, very prompt, stylishly dressed as usual. She had been in my office for about thirty minutes before I saw her, because of the necessary pre-screening papers that need to be completed and signed. When I was informed she had finished the paperwork, I walked into the reception area to greet her. She was not her usual bubbly self but was still very affectionate toward me. She gave me a big hug.

I took her into my office. I have a typical psychiatrist-psychologist office. I told her to feel free to sit anywhere she liked; she did not choose to lay down in the lounge chair, but she sat in one of my Queen Anne chairs, crossed her legs, folded her hands in her lap, and said with a sigh, "Well, I am here, what's next?"

I explained how my office worked and how I wanted to just talk in general about how things were going at home, how the ministry was doing, and how she was personally doing. I explained to Terri that she could begin talking about anything. She said, "I am doing well. My children are doing great in school, and the church is growing. We have so many new people—young people who are so eager for the word of God. So, for all practical purposes we are doing well."

Pastor Terri then turned toward the window away from me, gazing out of it for a few moments and said, "I don't know what else to say." She turned around slowly and said again, very quietly, with tears running down her face, "I don't know what else to say."

I said, "Pastor Terri, what else do you want to say? Is there anything else you want to say about the church, the children, your home, your husband?"

With tears still running down her face, she shook her head, indicating, no there was nothing else.

I told Pastor Terri we had just gotten started, and although I wanted to talk in depth about each area of her life, I would not talk about anything she didn't want to talk about. I wanted to know what was off-limits, and I would respect her wishes. Pastor Terri said very quietly, "Nothing is off-limits." She explained she was there in hopes of getting some direction and some help. She explained that probably the best way to proceed would be to ask her some questions.

I told Pastor Terri that there was a domestic violence support group in Miami Beach not far from her church. They were very discreet and had been very successful in helping young women who had been in abusive relationships. I asked Pastor Terri, if she was familiar with the organization and to my surprise, she said she was — not for herself, but she had referred members from her church to that support center. Pastor Terri explained they had a referral program in place at the church to help women and others who needed assistance outside of the spiritual realm of the pastors. I asked Pastor Terri what she thought of the domestic violence support group. She said without hesitation, "They are an excellent group; they are very discreet." She explained she knew what they did for several members because the members would share the information with her; Pastor Terri thought they were excellent.

On that note, I just looked at Pastor Terri. I didn't know what to say. I did not want to appear surprised, because as a psychologist it was important that we not look surprised at what was said to us, so I just looked at her and said, "Do you feel this group could help you and your husband?"

Pastor Terri felt they might be able to help her, but it was just too close to the church. She did not want to go to a place she referred her members to but she was willing to go to another location.

I asked Terri if she had any idea why her husband acted so violent. Pastor Terri explained that he had not always been violent, but she thought it might be because she was not as educated as some of the members; that he thought he had missed out on something. Their church had a large number of degree-holding members. While Pastor Terri might not have a degree, she was as polished and as well spoken as any of them. She was self-taught, well read, and very involved with the performing arts and the art museums in the city of Miami. Pastor Terri went on to say that her husband may have been feeling trapped because he knew what a divorce would do to his church. He also knew how much the members loved Pastor Terri. Pastor Terri thought her husband may have outgrown her and may want someone else.

I asked Terri if she would agree to a divorce if that was what he wanted. "Absolutely not," Terri said adamantly. "He may feel trapped, but I'm really the one trapped." She explained that she put her life on hold having children and helping Pastor Larry build the ministry. Pastor Terri believed this was a phase Pastor Larry was going through and she had no intention of leaving her comfortable home so someone else could walk right into what she had worked so hard for.

Terri looked at me and said, "Mary, where would I go, how would I live? My entire life has been centered on my children, my husband, and this church. What would my life be without my husband and this ministry, which, by the way, is as much mine as it is his?"

"Pastor Terri, I don't have all the answers, but what's most important is the safety of you and your children. I don't know what type of danger you may be facing in the house. I don't know if you are close to the edge and need to be removed from the house immediately for you and your children's safety.

If you do not believe you and the children are in any danger, then we need to think about a plan, which might include a vacation or temporary housing with family members; a period away from the stress. It may involve bringing in the house a mutually agreed upon family member to provide companionship and support. As we continue to talk with one another in our regular sessions, we will begin to put together a plan."

At that point, I realized that Pastor Terri had been in my office a little over two hours, but it had been a great initial meeting. I had a better idea of what was going on with Pastor Larry, at least from Terri's point of view. I was encouraged by the way Terri opened up and talked freely about her marital problems.

Terri had walked into my office a little uptight, but when preparing to leave, she had her shoulders relaxed and a more confident look on her face. She knew this was an uphill battle, but I really believed she was up to working things out. We certainly didn't solve all the problems, but we made a great start. I made a schedule for Terri to come in once every two weeks for one hour. I'd find another domestic violence support group that would accommodate Terri, one that was away from the church.

Terri did not have plans to leave her home, so I was not sure how much the domestic violence support team could do for her, but I had an obligation to make that referral. I didn't want anything to happen to Terri while she was consulting with me. She still needed professional assistance in making a decision as to whether it was safe for her to continue to live in the home. Although, I was well aware that Pastor Terri was going to do what she wanted to do, and she would not move out of her home on the advice of some outside group. It would have a lot to do with Pastor Larry and how he handled all of this. Terri did agree to speak to him regarding Pastor Larry having a conversation with me and/or one of the bishops from his denomination. I hoped he would be receptive. I thought it was a good sign that he didn't object to Terri seeing me after she told him what it was concerning.

In my next session with Pastor Terri, we would get into more detail as to when the abuse started and why she believed it was attributed to women who were educated at the church. I also wanted to delve deeper into her thoughts on why she thought Pastor Larry felt trapped. In the meantime, hopefully I would get a chance to meet and talk with Pastor Larry and his Bishop.

CHAPTER 7

Be The Best You Can Be

Sometimes you have to be better than That

As I reflected on Jane and her need for me to help her friends, I couldn't stop thinking about what troubled her to the point of wanting to take her life. Several things came to my mind, and I dismissed them, but one concern kept coming back and that was Jane's battle with her weight. I readily dismissed this because this was certainly not justification for suicide. Jane once told me that so many people were hurting because they couldn't control their weight, and it presented a real problem for many first ladies, who really wanted to represent the women in the church in a positive way.

As a first lady, I knew it was a challenge not to allow the close inspection of your members to affect your confidence and positive self-image. They watched you so closely; they looked at the color of your stockings, whether there was a run in your stockings, whether your stockings were sheer or thick. I remember someone commenting to my assistant about my ankles; they thought I had nice ankles. Who is looking at your ankles? I can only imagine if you were overweight, trying to find something to wear could be a problem.

There was one thing about Jane, although she was heavy, she knew what to wear, and she was always immaculately dressed. She loved linen and wore beautiful linen flowing dresses.

Jane talked to me about people she knew were depressed about their weight. She always talked about how difficult it was to lose weight. She had tried everything: natural diets, diet pills, Weight Watchers, Jenny Craig and a host of other programs I can't begin to remember.

Everybody loved Jane. I never thought about her weight because she was so loving and kind. Maybe that's the reason she never sat in the pulpit and was always sitting someplace in the audience. I just thought that was her way of greeting the people and being close to the people. I thought it was a great idea, and so did her husband. Was Jane suffering from depression because of the weight? Clearly her issues had to involve more than being overweight; that is not a reason to end your life, so that's why I dismissed the thought of her being overweight. Now I was not so sure.

She never talked to me that much about her weight. I knew it was a problem for her because she had made so many courageous attempts to lose the weight. Ron, Jane's husband, was very lean, an avid golfer and exercised at his gym on a daily basis. Jane went to the gym occasionally but not very often; she seemed to be embarrassed to put on her workout clothes and go to the gym, and that's why she tried so many other programs. Jane wasn't a quitter. At one point, I remember her going back to the gym.

She had a trainer for about six months; I never knew what happened with that. He might be able to shed some light on her state of mind. I felt so helpless. I should have been the person she confided in about her weight; she mentioned it to me, and I should have taken the lead, but I didn't know it was such a problem. I never gave it a second thought. As I think back, Jane was very overweight; she probably weighed about 200 pounds, and she was only five foot four. Everybody that knew Jane never saw the weight because she was so beautiful inside. She dressed extremely well and always looked immaculate. She mastered the art of wearing the appropriate clothes to hide her weight. She was very stylish.

It is so difficult to believe she felt so bad about her weight that it took her into a major depression. I just didn't see that. Usually, when someone becomes depressed you see or hear changes in lifestyle. I did not see any of this in Jane.

I have counseled many clients in the area of depression. Most people feel anxious or depressed at times. Losing a loved one, getting fired from a job, going through a divorce, and other difficult situations can lead a person to feel sad, lonely, scared, nervous, or anxious. These feelings are considered normal reactions to everyday life stresses.

But, some people, experience these feelings daily or nearly daily for no apparent reason, making it difficult to carry on with normal, everyday functions. These people may have an anxiety disorder, depression, or both. I didn't see this in Jane. I know sometimes she appeared overwhelmed, but we are all overwhelmed every now and then.

I have treated major depression. It is a treatable illness that affects the way a person thinks, feels, behaves, and functions. There is a small percentage of people that suffer from major depression; there certainly is a life-threatening risk for a small percentage of those that are unable to deal with life's issues. Could this weight problem have caused Jane to suffer from major depression?

I just didn't see that. Although I didn't see Jane that much, we talked every day, so how she acted and behaved in normal circumstances at the church, I didn't get an opportunity to observe. Regardless, I should have picked up something over the phone. But Jane was good at keeping a positive attitude about anything and everything, so I guess over the phone it was easy to disguise feelings and behavior.

If this was an area she was seriously dealing with, she never mentioned it. She shared with me that so many first ladies were dealing with a weight problem, but the ladies in her suicide note she asked me to help did not have weight issues. Maybe Jane felt, because she tried so hard with so many people, this was an area that was too difficult to tackle. At least, she may have felt that way when it came to her. The weight problem may be the most serious of all the issues mentioned by Jane.

I wondered if the reason Jane gave me the assignment she did, with these friends, was because she felt I couldn't help her friends with their weight. I could not help my friend that I knew was reaching out to me. I missed it. Was I too occupied with my own problems? Jane was always good at trying to help others with their problems. It is easy to get wrapped up in oneself, but she was always interested in helping others.

People needed to understand, including Pastor Terri, Evangelist Elona Braggs, and the other ladies that there were some things we could change. There are many things we can't change, like the color of our skin or our pedigree. We must strive to be the best we can be and sometimes, we had to be better than that. How is that done, well, one step at a time, with a made-up mind.

As a First Lady, I often told others we had to be the best we could be and sometimes we had to be better than that. *We can do all we can, and then we have to lean on God to take us to that next level, but we have to do our part. As a pastor's wife, we must live a balanced life. We have to work at this as leaders.*

I was speaking at a women's conference, when I was asked to elaborate on how to keep or bring balance into my busy life as a Pastor's wife, I shared my thoughts:

"We should all exercise in some way to keep in shape, whether it's a five-minute walk to start or just standing up and sitting down five times. We have got to start somewhere. We have to be conscious of what we put in our mouth. Every time we sit down to eat, we must concentrate on what we are about to eat.

Our mental state of mind is important. We all want a sense of wellbeing, being able to function and feel confident in our day-to-day activities. We can do some very simple things to help us in this:

We must develop and maintain relationships with people who support us and have our best interests at heart. It may not be easy, but if we look hard enough, we can find good people who care about our wellbeing.

It is sometimes hard to take personal time for ourselves because we spend every waking hour in church most of the days of the week. We never spend personal time with the family. There are simple things we can do: take a walk in the park, do interesting activities with our children and grandchildren, and go on a vacation. Many church people don't go on vacations because too much is going on at the church. We never think about vacations. Pastors and first ladies have just begun to take vacations, and some pastors are taking off a month.

Continue healthy relationships outside of the church– many of us were once part of sororities and fraternities, but someone told us that it wasn't Godly, so we discontinued our interest with these groups. We should continue these relationships outside of the church or nurture and cultivate new relationships.

Get involved in cultural activities. How many of us have season tickets to the symphony or the theatre? There is clearly a need for other activities outside the church. This is hard, but it is great for our mental health.

Most church leaders are active in their community, but sometimes we are so busy doing church work that we forget the church is also outside the four walls. We have an entire community that not only needs saving, but also needs help. We must establish urban initiatives that include our entire community—not just our denomination, but with whoever lives next door and down the street. We must volunteer our time to help others. We help the homeless and feed those who are in need at the church, but we must continue to build on what's needed in our communities.

A major problem is that we don't take care of ourselves. Sometimes we tend to let ourselves go and neglect our bodies. We have a responsibility to so many and we should get needed rest, exercise, eat properly and get regular medical exams. If we believe "The Body is the Temple of God" we must act accordingly.

As a first lady, we must be spiritual. I don't believe this is a problem for most in ministry, someone that prays on a daily basis, asking for God's guidance. The problem is found when the first lady has been so neglected that it is hard for her to pray; she feels separated from the ministry, and begins to doubt whether this is the place for her.

Pastor Patricia, the attorney from Houston, was such a woman. Jane talked about her often. Patricia Harris is one of the first ladies Jane asks me to counsel with and I am looking forward to meeting with her.

It is so easy to drift into a depressive state. Am I my brother's keeper? Yes, I am. We have to not only care about one another, but we must care what *happens* to one another.

Many have experienced so much hardship trying to be the best they can be. But, as I tell my clients, there is so much under your control that could change your life forever. Your life could change drastically. Whether it's your weight, your educational status, your job, how you dress, how you keep yourself up; if we take time to focus attention on ourselves, we can literally change our lives. It's important!

We have a tendency to sit around, particularly first ladies, and feel that our lives have grown stagnant, but as I have told many, you have your entire life ahead of you. We sometimes feel like we are in a rut because we think we have no control, but that is far from the truth. I've told my clients that, "we have control over who we are and who we want to be. No matter what your age, you have the capability of being the best you can be, and sometimes you have to be better than that, and that's when God steps in and takes us to that next level. I believe things happen beyond our wildest dreams when we take steps to make our lives better, and in turn it makes the First Family and many of those in the congregation's life a little better. It's like a chain reaction.

What inspires you to be the best will inspire others because first ladies are givers and will share their thoughts, their dreams and their aspirations with those who want an opportunity to also be the best they can be.

If we can embrace the truth that we can do all things through Christ, a truth that strengthens us, our lives will change for the better. This statement has never been truer. We must meditate on the word day and night. It's time that you feel comfortable in your own skin. You are not just First Lady, or Mrs. John Doe; you are Jan Doe, with skills independent of the pastor or the church. We have many responsibilities as First Lady and as pastors' wife, but it would be an injustice not to take time and put some attention to you.

When is the First Lady ever first? Well, that may be up to you."

CHAPTER 8

Discovering My Purpose

What about Me

$\mathcal{I}$ was relaxing in my home office, sitting in front of my desk, with notes everywhere regarding the major project involving Jane's friends.

When I thought about these gifted yet troubled ladies, I found myself searching my heart, my soul, every part of my being, wanting to know, why me? I had a life that was already full of clients. I had a family and a church family. I was also a first lady, one who didn't have a very good track record of supporting her husband and the ministry.

As I gazed out the window, I was finally able to focus on my own issues, my hurts, my fears, my aspirations. Then there was a calm that came over me. I realized that sometimes there was no one with whom to share your insecurities, your fears, and your hurts. I thought about these ladies, particularly Patricia Harris. In many ways, we were alike. Here I was with a need and a want to be more than first lady—is that so wrong? Being first lady can be a full-time job and for some, that's enough.

I thank God for a husband that supported me in my goals and aspirations outside the church. But I never forgot the fact that his first love and his first love for me was serving in ministry with him. As a psychologist, my job is full-time. I don't know how to make it part-time. I am also the first lady, and that's a full-time job as well. It was really difficult, but I made a commitment to the ministry and to my husband. I probably should think about slowing down my business, but that doesn't seem to be an option unless I close down my practice altogether.

Trying to schedule my time in my office, to my family, to the church and to these four ladies was mind-boggling. Frustration could easily set in if I weren't careful. I had so much to do, and I could feel procrastination setting in. I have a serious problem with procrastination. I organize my desk; I set goals and objectives, and I am so busy organizing that sometimes I can't get started—and I am the psychologist, so I can only imagine the problems of many of my clients. If they heard me talk like this, I think they would find someone else to tell their problems to once they realized I have so many of my own.

This request from Jane to help her friends involved more than just consultation. Although all of the first ladies seemed very kind, I planned to approach each of them and offer my services, which they may not want.

I thought back to a time when I was preparing box lunches for the homeless with one of the first ladies from a sister church. We were in a portion of the kitchen separated from the others when we got on the subject of people's expectations. She stopped what she was doing briefly, turned to me and said, "Many people will never understand how you feel, and it's important that you not share everything with everybody about where you are and how you feel, because they will never understand. They don't have a clue that you have some of the same issues that everybody else has. But sometimes we have to encourage ourselves; we also have to understand that God placed us here for a specific purpose. It is no accident that we are right where we are and doing exactly what God has placed in our hands to do." I knew I would carry those words with me and I have to this day. *The Purpose Driven Life* by Rick Warren was helpful in understanding the importance of knowing my purpose. The urgency of my calling was never so clearly communicated to me. Around that same time in my life, a senior citizen who was a member of my church said, "Pastor Mary, whatever you do, don't let time run out on you."

Coming out of that season, I believed I understood my purpose and I also understood the need to act expeditiously. I made every effort not to procrastinate; life is only that dash between our date of birth and our date of death, and it has to mean something. Our contributions to our family, to our community, to our church, and to this country have to mean something. I still find myself praying more often than not, "God help us understand our purpose, help us understand that it's not all about me and what I want; it's so much more." When you have an opportunity to touch lives and make a difference in someone else's life, brings joy to a family simply because you showed up, that's what it's all about. Sometimes we have to just show up. It may not be enough, but it definitely is a start.

With all of my own issues, I had to remember that I was just as human as everybody else. I really wanted to make a difference while on earth and I didn't know how I was going to do it. I was really working hard with my church and many of our ministries, and for me that certainly made a difference because it made a difference in the lives of others.

I needed to do everything I could to reach Jane's friends. Jane believed their issues were serious and she didn't want anything to happen to these ladies. I believed that if I could reach these first ladies, I could not only make a difference in my life and their lives, but in all the extended lives they are associated with through their churches and their ministries.

I thought it was interesting that Jane asked me to talk with Elona Braggs because she wasn't a first lady, but I understood involving Elona because she had a ministry that touched so many lives, and she had to be so many things to so many people. It was almost as if she didn't have a life because she was being pulled from so many different directions.

As a first lady you are a meaningful part of the ministry, recognized as the first lady of the church, but it doesn't always come out that way. I know for me, sometimes I felt like I was being tolerated because everybody was trying to get to my husband, the Pastor. I always waited patiently until the ladies hugged and kissed him; I waited till they finished looking into his eyes. I continued to smile. Some of the members never looked in my direction, they never attempted to speak to me but, of course, I am only the first lady.

Elona really was the only person in her ministry to focus on, but I guess after people have been prayed for, counseled, and you have given all you can give, you are totally drained, and people just move on. It can be a very lonely life. As I thought about Elona, she seemed very lonely; we were so surprised that we were the only people at her home after she ministered in Miami. She seemed so lively on stage, but her home had no signs of life. There were pictures on the wall but no family pictures. The condo was beautifully decorated. It was obvious she had used a professional designer. Although the colors of the walls made for a warm space, the overall décor was cold and impersonal. If it were to stand as a representative of its owner, one would truly believe Elona was as cool and aloof as her public persona. I chose to believe that because it was a place she kept for her visits in this part of the country, she didn't feel the need to invest the time it would take to truly make it a second home.

Ministry can be a very stressful commitment, not only for the First Ladies but their husbands as well.

Pastors and first ladies know all too well the need to encourage yourself. Counseling, the majority of the time, goes one way and that's to the members in the pew and the others that drop by pastor's office that need help, or the calls that come all night long from across the globe. Everybody needs help.

Pastors need encouraging, and First Ladies need encouraging. That should always be remembered. When people would tell my husband and me that they were praying for us, it was huge, and it encouraged us. It was exactly what we needed.

Many times the bishop, the pastor, and the first lady must encourage themselves. Sometimes, a member would come in and talk with me who was especially sensitive, and before they began to discuss their personal business they would ask me how my day was and sincerely inquired about my family.

I always found it particularly endearing if a member, sensing that my husband was tired, would purposefully keep their conversation short. It did my heart good and lifted some of the burden to see even one person give my husband such thoughtful concern.

If you call the bishop, the pastor or the first lady on Monday at 7 a.m. just because you are at work, think about how insensitive you are. Monday is usually an off day for most of our leaders in ministry. Your first words are, "I hope I didn't wake you." You wonder why first ladies are so protective of their husbands—they see how they are taken advantage of and you think she is trying to be unkind.

David encouraged himself in God, and that's what we have to do. He did it through praise and worship, and what better way to encourage yourself?

I am a psychologist, but I am also a first lady and we carry so much on our shoulders. Although many of the issues my husband deals with are not directed towards me, I feel the heaviness on his heart, and I see the wear and tear in his eyes when the day has gotten too long. The day never ends for him, and my heart goes out to my husband. I become very defensive when it comes to him. first ladies have to protect their husbands because the office visits, the home visits, the calls, the counseling, the hospital visits, the dinners, the speaking engagements just don't stop. They go on and on and on.

Sometimes, I've had to walk lightly at home. As a Pastor, my husband has dealt with so much, by the time he gets home, he's had enough. As a young pastor's wife twenty-five years ago, I didn't realize this; when I got home from church, I wanted to load him up with all the things that were going on with me. My husband would listen attentively and nod occasionally, ask a few questions, and I was satisfied. As I got older, I realized he was so worn out that he needed some space when he got home from church. He didn't need to hear me complain about the women. He would always listen attentively, nod, and ask a few questions. I realized that was for my benefit, but he really needed to rest and was not interested in some of the petty discussions I would engage him in. I learned to give him that needed space. I would encourage his heart through positive conversation when he got home from church.

I came to realize my job was to bring comfort to him after a long Sunday or a long day at the office. My job was to lift him up.

CHAPTER 9

We Chose Not To Throw Him Away

The Struggle

I had been so busy meeting with Jane's friends and my other clients, there seemed to be no quality time left for my husband Jonathan. I really felt the need to get away with him and my son, who Jonathan blessed me with from his previous marriage. Jake might have been my stepson, but I couldn't love him more if I had him myself. He was such a great kid; I had always just considered him my son. Jake was sixteen years old and lived with us. We had not had one minute of trouble with him. We were a little concerned because he had never exhibited an interest in girls or talked to us about anyone in particular. When the Junior Prom was about three months away, I asked him if he was going and he said he didn't think so. I asked him if he knew a young lady he would like to take to the prom, and he said maybe. I wanted to sigh in relief. I then asked him her name and if she was in any of his classes. He just looked at me and said slowly, "Her name is Britney, and we are in math together." He looked very strange, as if he was making it up. I said okay, and I started doing something else. I knew then there might be a problem. I didn't want to even say out loud what I thought.

I realized that my first thought regarding Jake's sexual preference was the effect it would have on our church. What would the members say? How transparent should we be regarding our son's personal life? I knew it would be naïve to think I was the only mother and first lady to have this type of challenge, but I was struggling with how to keep my beliefs from causing division within my home. As much as I wanted to preserve my relationship with Jake at any cost, it wasn't worth his soul or the souls of those we gave him responsibility over as a youth leader.

I missed Jane. I wish my friend was here to help me sort through some of these thoughts running through my head. She would never know how much of a hole she left in all of our lives.

I am not sure how I would feel if, in fact, he was gay. We were never unclear about our beliefs on the subject of homosexuality. We never shied away from teaching that the sexual act between those involved in a homosexual relationship was wrong because it was never a part of God's plan. When I teach the younger teenagers at our church I have always tried to make it clear that sex is a gift God gave us during our marriage. It is a blessed act by God between a man and a woman in a committed relationship bound by their covenant with God and their vows to one another. God gave us the purpose of sex– procreation, pleasure and communication with our spouse. He spelled it out for us in His Word. In regards to procreation – in Genesis 1:28 God blessed them and God said be fruitful and multiply and replenish the earth... The pleasure -spouses are blessed to find with one another is described beautifully in the Songs of Solomon, and communication- is outlined in 1 Corinthians, Chapter 7. It's important that Jake understands this is God's way.

In practical terms, the homosexual lifestyle precludes the continuation of the family God intended. Now, I have been preaching this to these young people year after year; my son was right there listening attentively. I have never had anyone close to me who was involved in this lifestyle. It's one thing to teach about homosexuality, but it's another thing to have to deal with it, up close and personal.

My husband talked with Jake and Jake admitted he was gay and has known he was gay for about three years, since he was thirteen years old. He told his father he had his first experience with a boy when he was fifteen and has continued to have relationships with boys at a nearby school. He has never been involved with anyone at his school because he didn't want it to get back to us.

Sometimes, you find kids who are desperate to fit in, so they do whatever they have to just to be a part of the crowd, but Jake is a leader. He has never followed anyone, so how did all of this happen? Jake and I talked that morning after my husband explained to me how their conversation went the night before. I couldn't wait to find out what was going through his mind. When Jake saw me, he knew I knew, and he walked up to me and gave me a big hug. Jake is about six foot one, very handsome, and very manly in so many ways, and I realized that was what threw me off. I knew he loved being in the kitchen with me, and he could make cookies better than most women I knew, including me, but he wasn't a wimp.

As the First Family of the church, it was very difficult dealing with major issues when you knew, although personal, would affect the entire church family.

Jake and I had the most wonderful conversation. He explained how he really tried to get involved with girls, but it never felt right; it felt very awkward. He just liked being around boys. He played basketball, and that was where he met similar young men like himself from a nearby school. He said they just clicked; he felt comfortable even though he knew this type of relationship would get him in trouble with us. He could not understand why this was so wrong when it felt so right. It was not just sexual attraction, but the depth of the relationship and friendship he was drawn to have with a particular person and wanting to be close to a particular person, how could that be so wrong? He actually prayed to God and asked God to take these desires away from him if they were wrong. He said his feelings were stronger than ever. I explained to him that we taught against this, and we believed it to be wrong.

Jake was raised up in our church, and he knew the Bible; he knew how to pray. I had to leave this in God's hands because there are some things that only God can do. Jake is the only child we have. Although I am his stepmother, he is my son, and my husband and I love him very much. I will continue to love my son, and although we don't support his choices, we love him, and we support him in every other way. We chose not to throw away our son because we love him, and he is God's creation.

Jake is bright and intelligent. He had always been active in the church. He played the drums for the youth choir. He was a leader in all of the youth activities, and he made all the meetings. I confidentially talked with one of the leaders in the church about Jake and was told that most of the members knew about Jake; and about others in the congregation who were homosexuals. I was shocked. I had no idea this was happening in our church.

Well, I knew as the First Family we had to confront Jake regarding his involvement in the church. We were torn with how to deal with him being in a leadership role. Should we take away his leadership roles, stop him from playing the drums with the youth choir?

My husband was so upset; I knew I was going to have to talk with Jake because whatever we did, we must show love. It was difficult right then for my husband to show love. I knew he loved Jake, but he was hurt, embarrassed, and frustrated with what he called a distraction. I explained to him this was not a distraction; this was our son that needed our guidance. Jake could feel the tension in the house, and he felt uncomfortable. He began to stay in his room, and wouldn't come out until he knew his father had left the house.

I told Jake I needed to talk with him, so we sat down in the backyard. It was warm, but there was a nice breeze.

I asked Jake if he remembered my teachings on homosexuality, and he said he did. I ask him if he remembered that this was a sin. He explained he didn't think it was a sin like the other things that were taught: thou shalt not kill, steal or do terrible things to one another. He explained, "I am not hurting anyone, and I am trying to live up to what's in the Bible the best I can."

Jake seemed so compassionate and sincere. I expressed to him that homosexuality is a sin, and we do not condone any sin. I explained that the word of God requires that if we love God, we cannot love what God hates. God hates unrighteousness. There isn't an exception for homosexuality because it seems popular or because we are seeing it more on TV. Sin is an offence to God, and he requires we repent of our sins.

Jake wanted to be clear. He asked me, "Are you saying I cannot play the drums in the youth choir, and do I need to give up my office in the youth department?"

"I don't have the authority to give an exemption to people who do not obey God's word. We believe these are the requirements mandated by God," I said.

Jake explained to me that this is who he is, and that would not change.

"Jake, if that's your decision, then you have made the decision to give up your leadership roles in the church," I said.

I made it clear to Jake that we loved him, and we would continue to affirm him and bring him to the truth, but we had to be faithful to our calling. We could not give an exemption to our son.

At the same time, it was important to let Jake know that although he could not continue in the leadership role at the church, we loved him and supported him in all of his activities at school and in all other extracurricular activities.

I explained to Jake that we would continue to pray for him that his eyes might be opened to the way of holiness. I explained he couldn't invite these friends to the house because we do not condone his lifestyle. Jake's social life outside of church, school and the house were limited unless accompanied by one of us or other adults we knew. My concern was that he was sixteen years old, and I didn't want him to get mixed up with an older crowd. I didn't know any other way to try to protect him. If he were 18, my thoughts would be different regarding curtailing his social interaction with others.

I was so concerned about Jake. He was a good kid, and I didn't want him to feel isolated and alone. I knew curtailing his movements was going to be a problem for him, but for his sake I didn't see any other options. Jake wasn't handling this well. He even implied he would run away. Now that was not an option. It was never clearer than at this moment that communication was a crucial key in not only preserving, but also nurturing our relationship with our child. It was important for us to be able to reach him no matter what problem existed. We couldn't even think of giving up. Prayer is our secret weapon, and we have to pray and continue to pray until things change.

When our children make mistakes, we have to always remember, nothing is too hard for God.

It is easy to dismiss what our kids are going through; try to cover it up, as if it isn't happening.

This was a difficult time for our family and the church. Our son had always been active in the church. We didn't want to discourage him and cause him to walk away from the ministry. What could we do to keep him interested in the church, and at the same time, drive home the point that there were certain things that would not be tolerated? We must maintain open communication with one another. It's important to be sensitive to Jakes feelings and at the same time keep the channels of communication open. I am committed to praying for Jake that God opens his eyes and his heart to making the right decision.

One of the biggest problems is older men who are practicing homosexuals in the church. Some of these older men are in key positions. How are we to handle this? This becomes a problem in our churches, when we are trying to discipline our young people, and they see those that are actually in high-ranking positions who are practicing homosexuals.

I talked to my son, explaining to him that he is our responsibility, and we must instruct him in the way of holiness. It was definitely one of those issues we would have to continue to pray for and ask God for direction.

I was really at a loss for words when my son wanted me to tell him the difference between him and Ellis North, who is the choir director, who Jake said was a practicing homosexual. How he knew this, I don't know. I explained to him that it's very important not to base these types of statements on rumors. If there is verifiable information, we should deal with the adults that are practicing homosexuals. These types of investigations in the church regarding homosexual activity should also require an investigation of heterosexual promiscuity as well.

Sexual purity regarding all the members, whether it was heterosexual or homosexual, would not be treated differently. If members were practicing impurity, that issue would be addressed, reprimanded, rebuked, and if necessary, disciplined. I explained to Jake that we were strongly against both impurities and it needed to be communicated through the teachings at the church, from the pulpit, in Sunday School, and in youth classes.

I am not sure if we could do any more than that without causing major chaos in the church.

I was concerned about my son and his personal lifestyle. I would continue to pray for him and give him direction. We would continue to pray for the church and those who need our prayers.

As the first lady of the church, it's important that we continued to show love not only to our sons and daughters but also to all of our members. We chose not to throw anyone away. We are all God's children with all of our imperfections. The church is a family with a pastor and a first lady; members look to us for direction on how to handle these sensitive issues. It's important that we start with our own family. This is an area that many pastors do not want to deal with directly, at home or at church, so the first lady, who many gravitate to, ends up dealing with many of the problems including this one.

I was wary myself, at first, as I tried to wade through the feelings of those who were struggling with their sexuality, but I quickly realized that God's Word, delivered God's way would not only illuminate and dispel confusion, it would cast out the doubt they were dealing with in regards to my continued acceptance of them as a lovable person. I understood that my job was to be there to listen, give insight and back it up with the unadulterated Word of God with a loving approach. I hoped that by quietly allowing those who wanted to share their struggles in these areas would be a huge step towards bridging any communication gaps that may eventually cause a division in the ministry.

There were several young men who shared with me confidentially they were struggling with homosexuality and I considered it a great start. I shared this with my husband, and he took over from there.

I wanted my son to know that he wasn't out there by himself. There were others struggling, just like he was struggling. Although he didn't admit he was struggling, God revealed that to me. This was a daily walk for all of us, and we would get through it together.

God loves each and every one of us, no matter what we have done and are doing. Some of the young men who were struggling need the shelter of the church more than ever. We must find a way to reach them, pray for them, and encourage them in the fact that God can do anything but fail.

It is a sensitive balance of preaching and teaching sexual purity, with regards to homosexuality and heterosexuality, and at the same time showing love and compassion to those who we chose not to throw away.

CHAPTER 10

What Happens When He's Gone

Preparing for the Inevitable

astor Alonzo and Plessey Humphrey lived in Detroit, Michigan. They never met Jane Steinbeck but had a mutual friend in Elona Braggs.

Plessey Humphrey studied with Elona Braggs one summer at the University of London, and they had been friends for the last fifteen years. Elona called me one day, and asked me if I had time to counsel this couple. She took time to give me the history of Alonzo and Plessey's relationship.

Alonzo was seventy-five, and Plessey was forty-two, and they had been married for four years.

Alonzo had been married twice prior to his marriage to Plessey. His first wife, Eleanor, died early in the marriage, and they had two girls together. Eleanor had cancer at forty-five years of age and died after four years of marriage. He had known his second wife, Larkita, for over twenty years; she was a member of his church. Although Alonzo had known Larkita over two decades, when they married he discovered he did not know her at all. Neither one of them was happy during the marriage, but they stayed together for eighteen years. Alonzo was an avid reader and a homebody. Larkita never read and loved going out and doing things with other couples. Alonzo did not like that at all but accommodated her. Alonzo liked Larkita and she liked Alonzo, but they never were in love with each other. They both agreed that the marriage was not working, and decided they would be happier living separate lives.

They agreed to sever their relationship and filed a joint dissolution of marriage based on irreconcilable differences. Larkita wanted to remain at the church because this was the only church she had ever known, and Alonzo agreed it would not be a problem since at the time of the divorce Alonzo had no interest in any other woman and had decided that he would not marry again. He had two girls from his first marriage and three children, two girls and one boy, from Larkita. Larkita helped raise his two girls from his first marriage, and everyone seemed to get along.

Plessey was a young girl when she joined the church, and had always idolized the pastor, and that's where her admiration stayed since she never thought she would one day be his wife. Two years after Alonzo's divorce with Larkita, Alonzo asked Plessey out to lunch, and the relationship began very casual and slowly. Although Plessey had always admired the pastor, she had never entertained romantic thoughts about him, so it took a little getting used to for Plessey. They continued to go out to lunch and dinner for almost a year. Alonzo asked Plessey to marry him, and they had been married for four years. Elona explained they were very much in love, but Plessey was very unhappy.

I was not exactly sure what kind of problems existed, but if I let my imagination run away, I could think of a ton of issues. I told Elona I wasn't sure if I had time; thinking to myself that I hadn't finished counseling Jane's friends, including Elona. Elona explained Plessey was contemplating leaving Alonzo. She said she loved him, but his five grown children were just too much to handle. Each one of them, except for the two whose mother was deceased, had this air of entitlement. It was clear they didn't get much attention from their father when he lived with them.

Larkita, their mother, continued to attend the church where Alonzo was pastor, along with all five children.

I guess the real problem was Alonzo didn't think anything was wrong, and probably would not agree to any type of counseling, particularly from a Presbyterian female co-pastor. Alonzo and Eleanor, his first wife, forty-three years ago established St. James Missionary Baptist Church, a now well-established church in Detroit. The pastor lost quite a few members when he married Plessey, but the church was still strong in the community.

I asked Elona why she was referring this couple to me. She explained, "If Jane had known Plessey Humphrey, she would have recommended that you talk with her." That's when it clicked, and I remembered that Jane had mentioned this couple to me in her letter. It's my understanding from Elona that Plessey is contemplating leaving her husband, and she is asking for help and will pay for any consultation in an attempt to save her marriage.

At that point Elona said, "This is my friend, who has been married to Alonzo for four years. I know they love each other. She has helped the church, and the members have grown to love her. I don't want her to throw away four years, and leave her husband who she loves and who loves her." Elona's voice was quiet and yet hopeful with her next question, "Do you think that love is enough for them to sustain their relationship?"

"Elona, I don't know, let me think about it," I replied. "You talk to Plessey and ask her if she is really interested in talking to a psychologist, and she needs to make Alonzo aware of this request as well, and find out whether he will be willing to talk to me."

Not three days later, Elona called and said she had talked to Plessey, and because Plessey loved her husband, she did not want to walk away from the marriage. She would welcome any help I might be able to give her. I asked Elona if she had any more insight on what was causing the problems. Elona said, after her discussion with Plessey, she discovered the issues had to do with the second wife remaining at the church, who had her own clique including her children. The two girls of the deceased wife had been very supportive and cooperative, and presented no problems. Larkita had two girls and one boy; her son was the oldest child, who attended the church as well, but not on a regular basis, and Plessey did not have very much interaction with him. He was cordial and had always been respectful to Plessey. I asked Elona, "Is Plessey serious about leaving?"

"Yes," Elona said, "She was definitely serious about leaving. She loved the church, but she couldn't control the backbiting and the sabotage encouraged on behalf of Larkita and her girls."

Plessey was a registered nurse and had worked as a surgical nurse for over fifteen years. She had planned to go to medical school, but it just never happened. She deeply regretted not going to medical school.

Elona said she had heard that Plessey got involved with Alonzo before he divorced Larkita and that it was a lengthy relationship. Instead of concentrating on going to medical school, Plessey was concentrating too much on her pastor. Although Elona didn't think this was the case, it was what was being whispered around the church.

If this was true, I didn't know how I could help Plessey. It seemed she had created this situation. If she had already asked God to forgive her, the question now would be whether she could forgive herself. It would be interesting to know if Larkita was aware of this relationship before the divorce; she probably was aware. It sounded like Larkita needed some counseling as well. Why would she want to stay at the church, not as the First Lady but as the former First Lady? What goes through a woman's mind that causes her to want to stay in the past, and have no desire to get on with her life? Well that's one way to look at it, but just because she wants to stay in the only church she has ever known with people who genuinely love her does not mean she wants to live in the past; it may mean she wants to live out her future in a comfortable and loving environment with church members she has known all her life.

Plessey called me and wanted to meet with me as soon as possible. She explained, "Elona shared with me what Jane said before she died about helping her friends."

Plessey was very moved by how Jane cared for her friends. I agreed to meet with her the next week because my husband had a conference in Detroit, and we would be there for three days. I thought it would be nice to have lunch with Plessey for our first meeting and she agreed.

Plessey and I met at a small café in Southfield, a suburb of Detroit. I thought we would do some small talk about the ministry, but Plessey jumped right in and said, "I never had any type of relationship with my husband prior to him being divorced from Larkita. I know there has been a lot of talk, but it is not true. We never even talked as if we liked each other before he was divorced from his wife."

I said, "Well, that's what people are saying."

Plessey said, "Like my grandmother used to say, 'you can't chase a lie.' I know the truth, and my husband knows the truth."

Plessey, I know the truth now and I am glad you shared that with me, I replied.

Plessey went on to say how much she loved her husband but how hard it had been trying to minister in that environment. "Alonzo," she explained, "Is a really good man, and didn't want to ruffle any feathers, so when he knew Larkita was doing something way out of line, he didn't say much. He said she had chosen to stay at the church, and they both agreed to remain a part of the church. She was his wife for over eighteen years and doesn't want to go anywhere. She agreed to the divorce because they just couldn't make it, and they really tried." Plessey went on to say, "I grew up in the church. I never considered the possibility of Alonzo as a husband, only as a pastor. I was like every young girl in the church; everybody loved Pastor.

When he and his wife agreed to separate and eventually divorce, it was two years after that date that Alonzo approached me, and we started talking." Plessey went on to say that initially she was very uncomfortable with him, but after a total of three years they decided to get married. Larkita never left the church, and because the relationship between her and Alonzo was good, there was no problem when he was single, but the minute there was discussion of marriage, everything changed.

Plessey said she believed Larkita thought he would never marry again because of his age, so she was very surprised.

Mary, Plessey continued, "I am not a jealous woman. I know my husband loves me, but the church is so divided. People are leaving the church because they think my husband should stand up to Larkita and their girls, but he doesn't. Larkita is now seventy-two, and this is her church home, and I understand that, but it seems as if she has her own women's department. She is teaching a Bible study class, and the few people that agree with what she's doing attend her Bible class, and they have nothing to do with me.

Some of the members still call her First Lady right to my face. That's just more than I can handle. I never get upset; I just continue to smile but I keep walking into situations like that, and there are many.

I have never felt like the first lady in this church. I feel like I am just being tolerated as his wife, and sometimes people act like I am not even there. I just continue to smile. Sure, I talk with my husband and he is very sympathetic. He apologizes for putting me in this situation. He feels that's about all he can do, short of tearing up his church. I certainly don't want that so most nights I just cry quietly until I fall asleep."

I had a very nice lunch with Plessey; I enjoyed her company and appreciated her sharing with me how she felt about her role in the church. I listened attentively because she really wanted me to understand the climate in which she had to operate in at the church. That picture was made very clear. She also tried to downplay it by saying things may not have been as bad as she portrayed them to be.

The majority of the people really did love her and worked with her on anything she did in the church. So it wasn't all doom and gloom; that just took place when Alonzo's ex-wife was involved. I was impressed with Plessey. She said some very nice things about Larkita; she understood how Larkita felt and apparently she was very uncomfortable as well. Plessey stated, "I don't believe she meant to be unruly." Plessey believed it was her children more than it was Larkita. Plessey shared that she believed Larkita was a kind person, and thought long and hard about where she would go at her age. She just didn't want to leave her church. A lot of people loved her at St. James' and that was where she wanted to stay. She had talked it over with Alonzo, and it was all right with him. His girls sang and played the piano, and he certainly wanted them to stay. As far as he was concerned it all worked out, until he got married again. Plessey said Alonzo had no intention of getting married again until he started talking with her.

Plessey was not working because Alonzo wanted her full-time in ministry with him. With all that was going on in the church, he wanted her down at the church every day. Plessey began to think about her future. Larkita seemed to be enjoying life. Pastor still paid all of her bills; she didn't work. This was one of the agreements outlined in their Divorce Decree. He was paying Larkita alimony through an agreement with the church.

Financially, things seemed to be going well now but what happens when he's gone. Plessey was concerned. Plessey did not work; she was like Larkita, but Larkita was much older than Plessey. Plessey was thinking ahead, and as a psychologist and a first lady, I have counseled many women in ministry with their husbands who were concerned about their future. Many times, it seemed the pastor put so much of his time and money into the ministry, there was nothing left.

A first lady does herself a disservice if she doesn't make an effort to understand some of the business of the home. The most important business is what happens to the first lady when he's gone.

She should know the answer to this question. She should know where all pertinent documents are located in the home or the church that pertain to her future when her husband passes away.

Plessey admitted she was thinking through what her life would be like once she became a single person in the church, and no longer the first lady.

She was thinking, "Who will I be then? Where will I go? If I remain in the church, where will I sit? What do they call me? Will there continue to be some type of recognition? What will be the dynamics between Larkita and me?

I understand more than anyone that the first lady is only first lady if she is married to the pastor. It is a life that depends on being connected to your spouse; sometimes that can be very scary. Your entire life is centered around this one man; people acknowledging you, giving you accolades—but what happens when he's gone?"

As the first lady, Plessey understood she had to help her husband determine her fate. She had to be prepared. She had to make sure he financially prepared for his departure, whether it was through independent insurance policies and/or agreements with the church.

As a psychologist, I talk to so many people, and I am aware of so many horror stories. When pastors die, sometimes, the first lady is left with nothing. Some wives have never paid a bill in twenty years. Every utility bill is in her husband's name, so when he dies, she is asked to apply for a new account in her name even though she and her husband have been with the utility company thirty years. She has no credit in her name.

It's important that the first lady doesn't let anyone determine her fate. I encourage the women to be prepared. I tell first ladies to make sure Pastor has prepared for them. Make sure that at least one utility bill and one credit card are in their name. If not, all of the credit cards you have enjoyed, once he dies, will be canceled because nothing was in your name, and you only had privileges to use the cards.

It doesn't take that much time to make sure there are adequate insurance or financial arrangements made through the church. This is how a first lady should be treated. Pastors get so busy with the church; they give everything to the church and forget the first lady should be considered even if she isn't first. She too has to live.

Last year, I participated in a panel at a phenomenal Women's Luncheon. Community, business, and religious leaders were invited to share challenges they'd noticed in their fields and solutions to some of those challenges. My topic was one close to my heart, as well as to a few of my friends and acquaintances at the time, because we had witnessed the devastation brought about by one of our friend's husband passing away and leaving her and her children with enough debt to completely alter their lifestyle. She wasn't ready, and he didn't prepare for her to outlive him.

I shared what I thought was a major burden placed on women leaders, and my impassioned five-minute speech kept tongues wagging for months. "It doesn't matter how old he is or how old you are," I stated, after one woman wanted to make excuses for not being prepared.

"Make sure your husband has adequate insurance as well, because when God calls him home, you are responsible for the funeral expenses. At a minimum, get a small policy for your husband's funeral. Make sure you have gravesite plots for both of you, expenses for your caskets, limos, flowers, and everything that is needed for the funeral. We sometimes forget to take care of ourselves, when we are so busy taking care of everybody else.

It's never too late to take care of this; make some inquiries, talk to someone in the congregation that has this type of expertise, and have them start on this right away."

This was the same advice I gave Plessey. She felt relieved because she had never thought about this, nor had she ever talked to her husband about these kinds of things.

Alonzo was old school; he didn't like to talk about these types of matters, but when Plessey shared her concerns, they went through the utility bills and put one in her name, which was based solely on her credit.

Although there were a lot of things going on in the church, Plessey felt so much more secure and took the attitude, "if I continue to love the people, God will take care of the rest." She made John 13:35 part of her daily devotions. She is standing on His word, loving His people, and trusting that as she surrenders her concerns unto Him, He is faithful and just to take care of her and her family.

It is so important to not only be prepared for when this day comes, but to be prepared in life as to what your plans are once you are no longer the first lady. Plessey was not working, although she had skills. She was very fortunate because her nursing background would help her secure a job. She had a bachelor of science in nursing, so she had a number of options. Before she left her area of work, she became a certified diabetic educator, a role that was always in demand. Plessey had thought about what she would do, and she certainly was better off than a number of wives in this situation.

Even if the first lady does not have a vocation or any skills, she should make sure her husband financially takes care of her so she will have some income when he's gone. A life insurance policy can take care of this. She should be proactive so that she doesn't have to worry about her future. Plessey was pleased that Alonzo put a financial plan in place for her future.

Plessey understood this was one less problem to worry about. Alonzo and Plessey were talking more about the church and about Larkita, and the best way to handle this difficult situation.

Our conversation helped Plessey understand there were a lot of issues and concerns to be worked out. Plessey made up her mind to continue to love Larkita, and reach out to her. She knew that was going to be difficult because although Larkita did not want Alonzo, she really didn't want anyone else to have him. Plessey had concluded that for the sake of the congregation because their needs were great, she was going to try to work things out with Alonzo.

I talked with Plessey and explained that Alonzo must do his part to make this a smoother transition for her. It would not work unless he stepped up to the plate and let Larkita know that Plessey as his wife must be respected. I have worked with many pastors, and for some there was always a problem being assertive when it came to the needs of the first lady.

The pastor, the shepherd of the house, leads even as he serves. The members look to him for guidance and watch for an example of how to treat each other as well as their leaders. The pastor in turn shows his members by example how to accept, embrace and love on the first lady. If he places her first in the presence of his members, that's what will be remembered when he's gone.

CHAPTER 11

When I Said "I Do"

Nothing prepared me for This

It had been about two weeks, and I hadn't talked with anyone. I still wanted to try to reach Patricia Harris. I had a phone number for her so I decided I would just call. Jane was very concerned about Patricia and talked often about the problems she had with her husband so I was very familiar with her issues, I just needed to talk to her directly.

Patricia and Gregory had a small church in Houston, St. Mary's Missionary Baptist Church with about two hundred members.

Jane used to talk about Pat, a very sharp lady who was a city prosecutor. Jane had told me Pat wanted to run for Attorney General for the State of Texas, a very high profile position. I didn't know what was going on with her now. Jane used to talk about how her church was growing, and how Pat was juggling her role at the church with her career.

Pat was about forty-five years old, and she and Gregory had been married twenty years. He never wanted her to take the job at the prosecutor's office, but Pat was so ambitious it was something she just had to do. Her marriage had not been good for a very long time. The members at her church loved her, and they loved to hear her speak, but her husband curtailed her speaking at the church. She was only permitted to speak if he was out of town or when an auxiliary had a special day or event, and they asked for her. Pat was certainly not looking for speaking engagements; she was so busy at work. If she decided to run for attorney general, that would take her away from Houston, she would have to live in Austin, the capital of Texas.

Sometimes she felt like her husband could care less, although he did not want her to run for office and did not want her to work at the prosecutor's office. According to Jane, Pat had asked her husband once, "What exactly do you want me to do? You don't want me to speak at the church; you very seldom let me have words, and you seem to always overlook me when you are thanking people at the church." She said, "he turned back to his work, dismissing me without an answer."

Pat was highly motivated; she loved her church and the people. She had stayed in her marriage because of their children, who were now eighteen and twenty, and for the church. Pat's father was a pastor, and she knew how important it was for the First Family to stay together. The women depended on the first lady, and they felt a sense of stability when there was a pastor and wife. Pat told Jane, she had seen too many broken First Families that destroyed the church because nobody was practicing forgiveness, and nobody was showing love. Jane said Pat was so compassionate, she told her "we all recognized everything is not going to be perfect, but it's important to see a First Family practice forgiveness and love. When there is discord in the first family, it hurts the growth of the church. Members know when there is tension or unhappiness among the first family".

Pat tried very hard to keep her family together, recognizing she had a husband who was clearly the pastor of the church, but had an overwhelming insecurity as to who he was. He scrutinized every compliment Pat received from the members, criticizing every move she made in the church. She had very little to say on Sundays because that was the way he liked it. If he knew that many of the members were there because of her, he would have likely been unable to contain his anger. Pat tried very hard to keep a very low profile at the church, but with her high profile job, it was really hard. Gregory wanted his family, but really didn't know how to feel comfortable with the achievements of his wife. He didn't understand that it made him look good.

I was not sure how I could help Pat; I didn't know of any other problems other than the insecurity of her husband. I called Pat and left a couple of messages.

Three days later, I picked up the phone. It took a while, but I got her at work. I was relieved when she told me she remembered me from the funeral. I hoped it would give me the open door I needed.

Pat Harris was a very busy lady. I could tell from her voice that she wasn't sure why I was calling. I wasn't sure she would be able to lend me enough of her undivided attention to allow me to explain my reason for calling her, but I'd gotten this far and I wasn't backing down.

I shared with her Jane's concern about her friends, and Pat was so moved that she said she would gladly see me.

She admitted there were some issues in her marriage that needed to be addressed. Communication between her and Pastor Greg had not been the best, and to keep tempers from flaring they had chosen to limit their conversations to the children and the ministry. The ministry was discussed less and less, because Pastor Greg did not want Pat to have much say when it came to the ministry.

I met Pat on a Saturday morning, bright and early; she flew to see me in Miami at her own expense. I was unsure how we were going to handle the long distance, but she had absolutely no problems traveling to me, and explained she would be happy to do as many sessions as necessary. She explained that she really couldn't speak for her husband. I had mentioned to

Pat that I really needed Pastor Greg at some of these sessions because a lot of the concerns had to do with him. She said she wanted to start her sessions with me, and we would see about getting Pastor Greg into the office. I even told Pat that I would be willing to travel to Texas for Pastor Greg. Pat liked that idea because she knew it would be difficult to get him to go anywhere for something like this. I told Pat that when I went to Texas, my initial meeting with Greg could be at a nice, quiet restaurant. Pat loved that idea.

I asked Pat to tell me a little about what she perceived the problem to be. In a very articulate manner, Pat said, "I know I am not perfect, but what is most disturbing is that Pastor Gregory's insecurity was not only focused toward me, but he has problems delegating to his leaders for fear that they may have better ideas than he does. He is highly critical of any idea if it doesn't come from him. He has stifled the growth of his leaders; consequently, it has flowed over into the congregation."

Pat said she tries really hard to smooth over the hurt and angry feelings of the leaders when he tactlessly criticizes them. In every meeting—not just some meetings, every meeting—if anyone had anything he believed was critical of the ministry, he jumped on the defensive very quickly. Some of the leaders who still spoke in the meetings and were not intimidated by his attitude, placated him by starting their sentences with, "Pastor, please don't take this as a criticism, but I think if we made just a few changes in our outreach, the ministry would grow by leaps and bounds." Sometimes this worked. Other times members would meet with him quietly and speak to him as though they were coming to him about an idea that might already be in his head so that he would be able to claim it as his own and move forward with it as though it were his own thoughts.

Pat explained that they had a great ministry, but many of the leaders had left the church. They couldn't deal with Pastor's insecurities. Pastor Greg was a good preacher; he knew the word of God, and was able to convey it in such a way that you always had something that you could take away with you when the service was over. She honestly believed that's why so many had stayed.

"Many of our members left and those that have stayed continue to hurt because of how he treats me," Pat said. "I am the co-pastor, and really should have a clearly defined role in our church, but I don't. Even if I were not the co-pastor, just the first lady, one would think this should carry some weight. With the women's department, I should be able to hold enough of a leadership position that I could see the vision of the Pastor reflected in the outreach and conferences we hold. It is as though he doesn't even trust me to represent him in this manner. I am not allowed to come up with a theme for the department of women at the church; he picks the theme, and he chooses the speakers that speak for the women's department. Where does that leave me? I tried so hard to be a team player, but he doesn't want a team; he wants followers to do exactly what he says.

I tried really hard not to show or express any type of discord between my husband and myself. As a preacher's kid, I know how closely the First Family is watched, so I am very careful with what I say and how I react to whatever he says or does. Body language is something the members watch. I know how they watched my mother when she wasn't all that happy with my dad."

I asked Pat about her job and her thoughts regarding running for Attorney General of Texas. At that point, Pat looked at me with such frustration and said, "I really want to run, and I have so many people in the state who want me to run. I am very active in the State Bar of Texas, and I am currently vice president of the State Bar. This has gotten me a lot of exposure, and I am known throughout the legal community in the State. My husband definitely does not want me to run, and I fear that I will lose my family if I make this commitment."

She continued. "When making this kind of decision, it takes the entire family rallying behind you, cheering you on. The commitment must be from the entire family, particularly my husband. If I run, I may lose my family, and we may end up in divorce court.

If that happens, it doesn't just affect me, but it affects our entire family and, equally as important, it affects our church family. There are so many people depending on us to be the stable, strong, committed family that we appear to be.

So Mary, tell me, with all your wisdom, what am I to do? Do I just stop practicing law altogether, and spend my time with the church? Keep in mind, my role is a background role because that's the way my husband wants it.

I love the practice of law. That's all I ever wanted to do, ever since I was a little girl. What am I to do, Mary? Don't get me wrong; I love my church, and I love ministry but my role in the ministry is so confining. I am so torn and so frustrated. Sometimes I can't stand to look at my husband. I think about walking away from him, taking my children if they want to go, and never looking back, but how many lives will I affect? Is this my lot in life? Mary, you are the psychologist, give me some words of wisdom, and tell me exactly what I need to do to have it all. [smile]"

"Pat, I wish I could just spout out some words of wisdom, and everything would be perfectly fine and everybody would be happy. There are multiple issues here, and many of the issues have been in existence from the inception of this marriage and nobody bothered to deal with them.

My initial advice to you, Pat, is to make no sudden moves at this point; any sudden move might turn everything upside down, and we know you don't want that. Pray about the timing of running for attorney general. Pray for direction regarding whether this is the best time for the family since there are other real serious issues on the table. Is it possible, based on what you know of the political climate in your state, for you to wait until the next term? These are just things to think about and pray about.

We have been together two and a half hours. Since you're here for two days, and we have another session tomorrow, I want you to think about your political career and its timing. Pat put some thought into how you would like for me to approach your husband. Would you like my first session with him to be a joint session?

Pastor Pat, communication is so important in relationships and I have found in all my conversations with pastors' wives that they tend to stop communicating with their husbands. Every first lady I have as a client has a communication problem with her husband. Why is that? Is there something about the nature of this profession that causes the pastor's wife to take a back seat in the ministry or the home?

Pat, don't misunderstand me; some of the strongest women I know are first ladies. They have to be so many things to so many people. Many work outside the home and they work in church; they are counselors to many of the women in the church.

I just happen to see those ladies whose plates are full and running over. Those who feel as if they are at the end of their rope and think there is nowhere to go but out the back door. I certainly want to be one of those voices saying you can make it, hang in there.

Pat, some things only come by fasting and praying. You have a God-size problem. You certainly should be an active part of the ministry with your husband. You should also pursue your lifelong dreams, if possible. You and Gregory both deserve to be a happy, and have a fulfilled life in the ministry.

Professionally speaking, Gregory needs to come in for about four sessions regarding his insecurity issues. He needs to work through some internal problems that he is attempting to deal with. Pat, it sounds like there is something else that's feeding his insecurity. I don't know what it is, but we have to find out what else is going on.

There is nothing more I can supply you with or advise you to do right now, other than to fast and pray."

Pat explained to me that it was going to be impossible to get Greg to talk about some of these issues, because he doesn't believe any of it was true.

She had plans to make an all-out effort to talk with Greg, and explain they needed help with their marriage, and they needed to address certain issues. I told her to let me know if there was anything I could do to help.

Five days later, Pat had her conversation with Greg about talking with me. Greg was totally against it. He told Pat that he was not going to talk with me about his personal business. He felt Pat's problem was that she wanted to be a workingwoman instead of the first lady of the church and his wife. He did not want Pat to work and continue to be married to him. Greg felt the ministry they were building was a full-time job and required two full-time committed partners to make it work.

He further stated that he was not going to talk to some stranger who was a friend of Jane's. As far as he was concerned, he couldn't trust my success rate with helping Jane's friends considering how Jane turned out.

"You tell me what you want to do," said Pat. Pat told me she had shared with Gregory, her desire to run for the attorney general. She explained she had a very good chance of winning. She expressed to him that the ministry was important to her, but she also wanted to continue her career in a way where she could help people on a larger scale and that this new position would give her that opportunity. She began to share the entire conversation with me, and my heart dropped lower with every word.

Pat explained to Gregory, "the church is a priority for me; I love our ministry, our people and all of what God has given us. But God has also given me the gift to be able to take on this monumental task, and I have the opportunity to tackle this with support all across the state. I have the support of Democrats and Republicans," she said.

She told Greg that she needed his help. She explained if he would just sit down and talk to me about their issues; she felt I could help sort them out. She asked him to talk with me.

Pat said he expressed under no uncertain terms, "I am not going to talk with her, and I don't think you need to go back and talk with her anymore either. I am against you running for attorney general, and as a matter of fact, you need to give up that job down at the prosecutor's office; we have too much work at the church."

Pat explained to Gregory, "If you would give me more freedom at the church just to help you carry out your vision, it would be different, but you close every opportunity to me. I would love to do more at the church if you would give me an opportunity to do more ministering. You act as if you never want me to say anything in a church service. I have to ask you if I can make an announcement, and the answer usually is no. Most of the time, you tell me to give it to someone else."

She further said to Gregory, "I am tired of living like this, under such a strain. It is clear we need help. Mary is willing to travel here to see you. Greg, if you want to save our marriage you will agree to see Mary. If you don't, I'm not sure if I can continue to go on like this."

She said Greg reluctantly conceded to give her more responsibilities in the church, but that he didn't see where there was a problem.

When she was done, her voice was almost lifeless. She didn't know what more she could have said to Greg to make him understand that she was being smothered by his overbearing nature.

She really didn't know what the next move would be. Pat explained that Greg was very set in his ways, and he was not going to change. He was not going to talk to me, and he was not going to cooperate with her regarding the church.

Pat was a very strong woman who loved her church. If Greg gave her the opportunity to play a meaningful, active role, her career would probably take a back seat to the ministry. To have an active career outside the church, and play an integral part in the church takes working together and supporting one another. I knew first hand that it could work. I was a psychologist with a full practice of patients every day. I had worked very hard, but

I couldn't have done it without the full support of my husband, so I really did understand the dilemma she was in with Gregory.

Pat did not want to lose on both ends. Her movements in the church were limited, and she didn't want to completely give up her career. Greg wanted her to stop working, but it just didn't seem fair. "If Greg would open up to you, Mary, that might help the relationship, but that's not going to happen," Pat said.

"Mary, I really could help Greg if he would let me. He is not a people person, so he keeps a distance from the people. Members gravitate to me, and Greg does not like that, but I am a people person, I love people.

As I continue to think about what I should do, I keep going back to my mom and dad. As a preacher's kid, I knew my parents were always concerned with making sure the membership felt comfortable and safe. It was always important to them that the First Family appeared to be together, even if they weren't. I really have a commitment to my church family." I heard Pat sigh over the phone line and my heart went out to her.

With sadness in her voice, "I have very little cooperation with Greg to pursue the attorney general position, there is no way I could successfully proceed. I am going to have to pass on that for this term. Maybe by next term we will have worked out a lot of these challenges in our marriage." Her voice became firm with the next sentence. "I am going to keep my prosecutor's job because I am good at it, and I enjoy my work. There must be compromise in our relationship.

Greg gives me a pretty hard time at church, but I am still the first lady. The membership loves me and I love them. That brings me great joy."

Later that week I could no longer ignore this nagging doubt I was having. I really wanted to talk with Greg because I felt I might be able to help him, but I had this feeling that Pat was not telling me everything. I made a call to Pat explaining I understood Greg did not want to talk with me, but I needed to know if there was anything else that was keeping him away from the two of them having a closer relationship. I remembered Pat explaining they had not been close for a couple of years, and as she continued to open up, I realized Pat meant there was no sexual contact between the two of them.

Pat wanted to meet with me because she said she needed to share some areas of concern that she purposefully had left out. We agreed to meet in a couple of months in Dallas, where we both would be attending a pastors' conference. Greg would also be at the conference, and there could be a chance for all of us to sit down and talk.

I had a suspicion that Greg either had issues with his sexuality or he had another woman. Pat was a beautiful woman. Why would he not be intimate with his wife, unless something else was going on? He acted as if he didn't want to lose her; he didn't even want her to work. But why would such a possessive man have such a poor relationship with his wife?

I was looking forward to meeting Greg, and seeing both of them at the pastors' conference in Dallas. Many of my clients would be going to the pastors' conference. It was an annual conference sponsored by Bishop Don Shapes. We looked forward to going every year. I knew Pastor Larry and Terri Jones would be at this conference because we had talked about it. I knew Elona Braggs would be there because she was one of the evening's speakers. I was not sure if Alonzo and Plessey were going. I believed financially they were having a difficult time.

The Conference was being held in September, in just two months.

A month before the conference, Pat called me and said she needed to share something with me. I reminded her that we would see each other in about a month at the pastors' conference, but she didn't want to wait. She would give me an idea of what it was now and hopefully, she said, we could talk about it more in depth when we saw each other next month.

Pat said that what she was about to tell me was very difficult; she said it was about Greg. She reiterated that he was a great man of God, but he had a demon that she believed would destroy him. I asked what it was, and she became quiet. After a few seconds, she almost whispered, "My husband is seeing someone."

Pat had discovered her husband had been seeing this person for over three years. She found some letters, and Greg didn't know she knew. I asked her if she knew the woman and Pat said, "I wish it was a woman, but it's not. It's a man, and I know him. He has been in our home, and he is a deacon at our church."

Then I got quiet. I asked Pat what was she planning to do, and she said, at this point, nothing. She'd just discovered it, and I was the first person she called. I told her, "Well, don't do anything or say anything. Wait until we can get together and talk, if you can."

She said she would wait because she didn't have a clue how to handle this situation. Pat explained she suspected something like this was going on, but she just wasn't sure. I asked Pat what made her think something was going on, and she said there were just little things she would notice.

"Mary, it has been an everyday struggle with my husband ever since we were married. Before we were married he was a totally different person. When we first met he seemed so eager to get married and start a family. He was excited about becoming a pastor, but he felt he needed a wife before he started the ministry. He knew my family, and he knew I was a preacher's kid raised up in church. He felt we were the perfect match. We dated for six months, and then started talking about marriage. I really liked him because he was such a gentleman; he never even tried to kiss me until two months into the relationship. I thought, wow, he is really a nice man. Although I was not head-over-heels in love with him, I knew he was a good man. He was handsome, and I couldn't believe someone hadn't grabbed him before now. He was forty-five years old and had never been married.

After we were married although he encouraged me to pursue my career, he told me once we got the church going, I needed to focus all my attention towards the church. I explained how my salary would help him while getting the church started. He thought about it and agreed reluctantly."

I asked Pat how she found out he was involved in a homosexual relationship. Pat said she was going through some old briefcases, trying to clean them out, and that's when she discovered the letters from a deacon in their church. Everyone referred to him as Deacon Turner. There were four letters, written at different times, but they were all in a manila envelope. Pat said she didn't have a clue why she opened the envelope. In the letters, Deacon Turner was expressing how he felt about her husband, and how he didn't mean to hurt Pat. She said she was so shaken she couldn't finish reading the letter, she just closed them up, and put them back in the envelope in the briefcase exactly the way she found them.

Clearly something was going on because Deacon Turner talked about being with him three years ago at the pastors' conference. It sounded as if that's where the relationship started.

I asked Pat how she felt now. She said she was just numb, but agreed again not to say anything until the two of us talked at the pastors' conference.

I hoped Pat could hold out. How do you tackle this type of problem? Was there hope of repairing this relationship? As a psychologist, I had encountered many different issues, but nothing like this. You not only had the First Family, you had an entire congregation to be concerned about. One thing I would never forget was that God can do anything!

CHAPTER 12

The True Way Trinity Church- Without Jane

Quiet Storm

*R*on Steinbeck, Jane's husband, was a very likeable guy. So when the whispers and rumors of the possibility of foul play started moving through the church community they quickly dismissed it, and stopped people from further spreading what they thought to be a vicious lie. They rallied around their pastor, but Ron was oblivious to most of it.

Ron was in shock over Jane's death and kept saying, "She didn't have to do this. She didn't have to do this," as if he knew why she did it.

Ron was a self-made man. He had a degree from a small college in Iowa, and went into law enforcement. He was a policeman for about five years, when God called him to the ministry. He'd always been a Bible scholar; he loved to teach Sunday School at a local church he attended in a little small town outside of Miami. He started the True Way Trinity Ministry with his wife, his oldest son, and three friends from the police department, and it grew. He and Jane worked hard to build the church and loved one another very much. Jane was the marketing and social arm of the church. She loved people and never met a stranger. When the church first started, Jane became intimately involved with all the members. She knew everybody's names and their children's names. It grew quickly as a family church, and Jane maintained that same personality where she didn't meet strangers, and endeared people to her family.

Ron was an astute businessman. He started buying up property close to the downtown area, which was a central location for them. By the time the membership reached about five thousand members, they owned the land and began to build this megachurch, which appeared to be way too big for the congregation.

Ron's background was Southern Baptist, and Jane's background was Pentecostal, so they had a lively church. Although the church was predominately white, every ethnicity was represented.

Ron was always home to have dinner with the family by 5:30 p.m. Jane didn't do much cooking because she had help in the home, sometimes just to cook dinner.

Their son, Bryan was seventeen and had frequent problems at school. He was very bright but a little unruly. Frequently, Jane would have to go up to the school and talk with his teachers.

Ron not only had a thriving church, but they had a production company that worked with other groups and a TV ministry. They'd gone with a friend's suggestion to have a travel agency housed at the church's location; although they didn't have a clue if it would be successful. It became a thriving business for the church because the majority of the members used its services the first time because it was part of the church, but continued to patronize it because they offered such great service.

A school was attached to the church, kindergarten to seventh grade. It was a private school, and although enrollment went up every year, they struggled to keep it open because they gave scholarships to most of the children.

The ministry was thriving, a very large church with a small-church feeling of family.

With all of the personal, business, and ministry obligations I didn't get a chance to talk to Ron as much as I wanted the week after Jane's death. When we did talk, I could tell he was still coming to grips with his wife's death.

One night he called me, speaking so quietly I could barely hear him. It sounded like his heart was bleeding. Knowing that I might have been the first person to speak to him about her in this fashion, I just listened. He murmured vaguely about something that only he and Jane knew. Something they had not shared with anyone. Ron said he thought this secret that they carried for so many years might have caused Jane to take her life. He started talking randomly about Jane and the secret.

I had shared my letter from Jane with him and I had no idea the statement Jane made about he and Bryan being ok without her would affect him so much. The night he called me, he asked me why Jane thought that he and his son would be okay if she were gone, but stated it in such a way that I knew it was a question he asked himself over and over. Jane was his rock; she was the stabilizing force that kept him and Bryan on solid footing. It was hard for Ron to even conceive how he and Bryan were going to make it without Jane. When I asked about Bryan, he was silent for a moment then said that Bryan was clearly a mama's boy, and he hadn't spoken to anybody since his mother died. I sat there and quietly took it all in until he was all talked out; then he hung up the phone.

On the surface, there seemed to be nothing wrong with the ministry. Those who worked in the ministry seemed to be a very congenial group. There were fifteen full-time employees, and everybody loved Ron and Jane.

The ministry had not been the same since Jane passed away. It had been eighteen months, and there was this void, this emptiness in the sanctuary on Sunday mornings. There used to always be a running joke with some of the members to see who could find the First Lady in the sanctuary. She would sit all over the place and say to Ron, "Try to find me next Sunday; you will have a hard time."

The members loved their first lady, because she seemed to always put them first. Jane used to tell the members to always love one another. She would talk on many topics, but her message always ended on loving and being kind to one another.

There remained sadness in the sanctuary, even though it had been a year and a half since she died. All of her pictures with Pastor Ron were still on the walls and in the offices. He acted as if she was still alive, talking about her every chance he got. Many women were trying to talk to him, but when they started a conversation, and he started talking about Jane and what a wonderful wife she had been and saying that no one could ever take her place, they backed off pretty quickly.

When a husband loses his wife of thirty-two years, and a congregation loses their first lady, the way they lost Jane, it's devastating.

Jane was such a rock for so many people. She was a woman of faith who believed in the word of God. She taught many of the young women how to live by faith. This was such a shock to the congregation they began to doubt some of the things they had been taught at Trinity. The church was a safe haven where they could go and be safe. Jane loved the people, and she made them feel safe and assured them that God would never fail them nor leave them. In a way, the church lost both of their leaders for a while. Pastor seemed to be waiting for something to happen, maybe for Jane to walk through the door one day.

He would show up to the office, but it was difficult getting any assurances out of him because he was walking around in a daze.

Jane as first lady of the church gave so much to the church. She undergirded her husband; she was a shoulder that so many leaned on and cried on. She gave direction to the women of the church; she was transparent when sharing with the young ladies the notion that they could live saved and free from sin. They might make mistakes, but if they had a desire in their heart to live a holy life, they could do it. Jane as the first lady brought a smile, a hug, and a sense of security to so many. Jane's Pentecostal background brought so much to the ministry. Her strong belief that people could live free from sin took the church to a whole new level. Jane spoke in tongues, but Ron never embraced speaking in tongues. She never stopped speaking in tongues, and talked about it often, and many of the members received the Holy Ghost and spoke in tongues. Ron never talked against it; his orientation was so different from Jane's, but she told Ron she was going to continue to pray that he receive the Holy Ghost.

Is the ministry ever prepared for this type of loss? It's one thing to lose your leader through sickness or an accident. But how do you come to grips with your first lady taking her life? No one knew what happened or why she was so distraught. Why didn't she believe what she preached? We put our leaders on such pedestals. The First Lady had real issues that needed attending to, and she wasn't able to get help. She was just a woman hurting and reaching out, in her own way, but no one noticed.

In thinking back to that late night call I received from Ron, it wan't long after that, I got an opportunity to sit down and talk to him about what happened. He seemed so much in a daze about everything. I asked him what happened, and he kept saying he didn't know. I knew he knew something. She had said as much in her letter, and even stated that at some point Ron would talk to me about what had happened. I explained this to Ron, and he just looked at me. He said he and Jane had been carrying this secret for over twenty years.

Ron wanted to open up to me, but he just couldn't. He said he needed more time so I didn't push the issue. Whatever happened, he said he thought Jane had gotten over it; they had talked it through many times, and she seemed to be getting better.

He felt she was coming around, and she would be all right. He said he even suggested she talk with me, and she had agreed to do that, but it just didn't happen. He said Jane's faith was strong, and she prayed continually about what had happened. Ron had really felt things were getting better.

I asked Ron how Bryan was getting along. He told me that Bryan was going to need help. He and Jane had a special bond and communicated well with one another. Ron said many times he felt left out because they seemed to get along so well; they were so close. Bryan had just closed up; he didn't talk to anyone. He would answer questions, but other than that he didn't say anything. Ron told Bryan he wanted him to talk with me. Bryan knew I was a psychologist, and he agreed, but never called me. I didn't expect Bryan to call; I would have to reach out to him.

I was really concerned about Ron. Although he appeared to be okay, I knew he wasn't. Jane was the stabilizing force at the church and at home. Although the ministry was large and they had a full-time staff, when there was a serious problem, the associate pastor would go directly to Jane, and she would handle it. Pastor was a great preacher but didn't do so well when it came to dealing with employee issues or general complaints. The associate pastor normally handled problems, but if it got serious he didn't hesitate to talk to Jane.

Jane had a heart of gold, but she was very business-oriented and could be very stern if she had to be. Ron said, "One day, one of the employees, Lynn, who had been with us for over fifteen years became a little unruly and felt that since she had all this seniority, she could pretty much do what she wanted. She was one of the secretaries, and she did have a lot of power when making appointments. One day, she was very rude to someone over the phone, and the person complained to the associate pastor. He tried to talk to Lynn, but she felt she was above him. The associate pastor called Jane, and asked her to talk with Lynn. This was not the first time Lynn had done something that Jane had to talk with her about. Jane went straight to Lynn, and explained the one cardinal rule was that she could not be rude to anyone, and she was not going to tolerate it. Jane told her, 'we love you, and you have been here longer than any of the other workers, but I am going to have to reassign you. You will no longer be the executive secretary in the pastors' suite; you will be placed in the typing pool. We will let you keep your salary because of your seniority.' Lynn was so upset she quit right on the spot, which was a mistake. Lynn discovered she couldn't find a job making the kind of money she made at Trinity, and asked to come back but Jane said no.

It was so obvious that Ron really missed Jane. He said, "Things seemed to be going so well for the church. It was a large church, but it operated like a close-knit family church. Trinity was growing. Jane had her hands in everything, especially the women's activities. The church was running like a smooth machine. The death of Jane was a major blow to the ministry. It hit us like a quiet storm, destroying everything in sight."

In time, I know Ron would share with me what actually happened to Jane.

CHAPTER 13

The Pastors' Conference

Secrets

*W*e had been waiting for this conference all year, and it finally arrived. My husband and I got to Dallas the day before the conference started. It was a full week, with great preachers from all over the country. There were wonderful workshops and great preaching. We would be busy the entire week. One of the highlights was Elona Braggs, who was the keynote speaker on Wednesday night of the conference. My husband, Jonathan was one of the conference speakers during the day. Pastors Larry and Terri Jones arrived Tuesday morning of the conference, and the four of us had a lovely dinner on Tuesday evening. Plessey Humphrey was in attendance, but her husband was not able to make it. Pat and Gregory Harris were also there. Pat was one of the workshop expeditors dealing with sexual misconduct in the church. I looked forward to seeing all my friends—yes, my friends. This had been an interesting twenty-two months, and I had developed wonderful friendships with Jane's friends. We were still working on our issues, and it was a continuous journey for all of us.

On Wednesday I talked with Elona. I invited her to dinner, and we were all looking forward to having a wonderful evening together after the Wednesday night service. She was really happy to hear from me. Elona was doing well; she had been traveling the globe. There was no special person in her life as of yet, but she felt good about herself. There was a certain confidence she felt that was obvious in her talk, walk, and even her presentations. Although she had always been a great preacher, she was now an even better preacher. We'd had several consultations. Every time she came to the States we planned a consultation, and it had worked out great.

The theme for the pastors' conference was, "Focus on Community and Branch Out." Evangelist Braggs spoke on branching out. Bishop Don Shapes host this conference every year and he introduced Elona. The place was jam packed. There was a praise team singing prior to her speaking. We had great seats thanks to Elona. Pastors Terri and Larry Jones, Plessey Humphrey, and Pat and Gregory Harris were also there. I had hoped at some point that we all could get together. I invited everyone to my home for the holidays to celebrate the life of

Jane, and they all agreed to come, so I really looked forward to the holidays.

Elona did an excellent job. Participants who attended bought every book and CD she had brought from London. She had to have additional product shipped overnight for the rest of the conference, which was no problem since one of her printing companies was located in the States.

She had been tremendously successful in the United States, and there was great demand for her throughout the country and abroad. The Wednesday evening dinner was my husband's second time meeting with Elona, while Elona and I had been together many times.

This was a tremendous conference; it allowed pastors and leaders of various churches across the nation to intermingle and exchange ideas and strategies in an effort to enhance the growth of their churches. The focus of this year's conference was for our leaders to reach out to the community, the city and the world. Specific directives were given in each workshop and night service, on how this goal should be reached.

In addition to this overall directive for the conference, there were workshops that focused on the mental health of pastors and leaders, and how to strengthen one another. I loved being a part of those workshops because it was a subject so often overlooked but so needed. There were always great presenters, and some had been psychologists like me. I had attended this workshop in the past as a presenter, and there were always great lecturers and good interchange between those that were in attendance. This year's workshops were no different. I enjoyed the sessions even though they struck a chord deep in me. It was hard to miss or dismiss the depression and the hurting of the pastors who were being transparent, and reaching and searching for answers. It was always a small workshop because many leaders didn't want others to see them attending this type of workshop. I believed those leaders and pastors who attended this workshop were those that were secure in themselves and wanted their ministries to go to another level, and at the same time, they personally wanted to be prepared. I loved it. Pastor Larry and Terri Jones took a special interest in this workshop.

My husband and I met Pastors Larry and Terri Jones for lunch on Thursday during the conference. Although we had met Wednesday night, we didn't get a chance to say much to each other. He knew who I was, and he also knew Pastor Terri had shared their problems with me. He was very cordial. We had a wonderful lunch. My husband, like Jane, doesn't meet a stranger, and you would have thought they had known each other for years. They talked mostly about the confer-ence, and how much they enjoyed being there. Pastor Terri and I talked about attending Attorney Pat Harris' workshop on sexual misconduct; she was an excellent speaker and presenter. They acknowledged they would be at our holiday dinner hon-oring Jane.

I got a small window to talk to Pastor Larry when my hus-band went to visit someone in the restaurant that he hadn't seen in a long time, and Pastor Terri went to the Ladies room.

I took that moment to request a meeting with him and Pastor Terri. I wanted to convince him of the urgency for the meeting in regards to working out the issues Pastor Terri had brought to me. Surprisingly, he said he didn't have any problem with that, and he would let Pastor Terri and I set the date and time. I was wary, but his body language indicated he was sincere about wanting to meet.

This was a great lunch, and we all enjoyed being together. I got a chance to see them several times after the lunch before we left Dallas. The lunch with Pastor Larry and Terri alone was worth the trip to Dallas.

Pastor Terri and I got a chance to spend some time with Pat Harris after her workshop. We met in a coffee shop, and talked in general about her workshop, and finally got around to talking about Jane and how we all missed her. Pastor Terri and Pat didn't know each other but saw each other at Jane's funeral. I, of course, did not discuss that they both were clients of mine, but I think they knew. I had told Pastor Terri earlier that I needed to talk to Pat alone sometime after her workshop, so Pastor Terri politely excused herself.

I looked at Pat and asked her if she was okay and she said, "No, I am not okay." Pat shared that she had a feeling Greg knew she was aware of what he was doing. She said, "He just started acting a little different. We were not that intimate before; maybe once a week, but even that stopped, which is what I wanted. I am not interested in being intimate with him. I can't stand to look at him. I didn't want to come to the pastors' conference but I came because I knew I would be able to talk to you and, of course, I was scheduled to do the workshop. The reason I am so upset is that I saw Deacon Turner yesterday, at this conference. I have never seen him at this conference before; he came up to me and spoke. I was so shocked to see him. I just looked at him, and I couldn't say a word. I just nodded my head and walked away. When I saw my husband later that day, I ask him if he knew Deacon Turner was at the conference; his eyes got big and he said, 'No, I didn't know he was here.' I didn't say another word. I just turned and walked in the opposite direction.

Mary, I didn't know what to do, I didn't want to go back to our room; I was just done. I knew I needed to go back to the room because the conference was no place to make a scene. I wanted to pack my clothes and go home. I had my purse and an oversize bag with me that I use as an overnight bag so it wouldn't be too obvious if I left him right now. I had to go somewhere and think. I left everything in the room: my clothes, shoes, everything, but I knew if I went back to the room, something might happen. I wanted to tell him to have fun with Deacon Turner, because I was going home." She looked at me with fire in her eyes, and her bottom lip trembled slightly. "Mary, he had the nerve to have his lover meet up with him at the conference and, I guess, he planned to sneak out and be with him and with me." She grit her teeth as she said the next line, her anger palpable. "All I wanted to do was get on the next plane to Houston, pack my things, get my children, and go to my mother's home. I didn't want to ever see him again."

I felt I had to intervene at this point.

"Pat, what about the church? You can't just walk away from the church. As the first lady, and you know better than I, as a preacher's daughter; the role you play is very important, and they will be looking for you. The members are not going to understand. Do you want them to know what's going on? How are you going to handle the church? Pat, I know you're angry, but what you have forgotten is your responsibility to the members. I don't think you can just walk away."

"Mary, what am I going to do? I can't live with him."

"Pat, I think you should stay here in Dallas at the conference. If you feel you have to get another room, do that, but you must have a conversation with him before leaving."

"Mary, can you tell me why Deacon Turner is in Dallas?"

"Pat, I don't know, but I do know what's at stake is not just about you and Greg. You have an entire congregation of members who are depending on their pastor and wife.

Of course, Pat, you are thinking what about me? What about your feelings? Unfortunately, in our position, responsibilities and obligations come first. What we want does not factor into some of the choices we have to make. It's not about us it's about the mantle God has given us. It's about his people; it's about souls being saved. He knows we are not perfect, but He has equipped us as his representatives. He chose us. We can never forget, He chose us."

I could see the inner war going on inside of her, but I had a feeling she would choose correctly. Pat knew she had to sit down and talk to Greg before she left the conference, and she had no idea what she would say to Greg. From what she had read and seen, all evidence pointed towards her husband not wanting her. He wanted a man. "As I think back over our life," Pat said, "he was so eager to get married because he wanted to start a church. That's the only reason he married me. He wanted to start a church, and he knew it would look better if he were married."

"Pat, you have two beautiful children, and I understand he is a great father to your children."

"That may be true, but is that what our relationship is built on, his relationship with the children? They are almost grown and will be leaving soon. Then what?"

"All I know, Pat, is that you need to talk with him."

By the time we parted, Pat had agreed to stay at the conference at least long enough to talk with her husband.

Pat and her husband had told me they'd come to my house for dinner during the holidays. Those plans may change. I hoped they would not change. I planned to talk with all the families at the dinner and share with them that Jane had written a letter and asked me to work with each one of them on various issues. I didn't plan to get into specifics, but I did think it was important that they understood how we all came together. I wanted them to know how much Jane cared for each one of them. The problems between Pat and Greg are the very reason Jane asked me to help.

As the conference came to a close, I had bittersweet feelings about the week. It had been a good conference, but my heart went out to Pat. I wasn't sure what she was going to do. I had just zipped up my jacket and was prepared to go down to breakfast when my phone rang. I saw that it was Pat. When I pressed the button to answer the call and heard the sound of Pat's voice on the other line, I knew something was wrong.

When Pat arrived at my room, she was visibly distraught, and once she stepped over the threshold, she began crying. I took her into my arms to comfort her and we walked over to the couch.

Pat began to recount what had happened. When she went back to her hotel room at the conference, she didn't say much but that wasn't unusual for the two of them. Greg made the reservations, and he also made sure he got two beds in the room, so Pat didn't have to worry about getting too close. Pat went on as if nothing was going on. She wanted to watch Greg's movements during the conference. Sure enough, for a couple of days and nights he was totally out of pocket. Pat couldn't find him anywhere, and didn't see Deacon Turner either. She didn't say a word to him until that morning when they were getting ready to leave. They were packed, and sitting in the room, and she asked Greg where he was when she couldn't find him on those two different occasions. He told her he didn't know what she was talking about, and started reading a book. I told him, "I know you are sleeping with Deacon Turner. I know all about your affair with him for the last three years."

Pat said, "He didn't say a word.

You don't have to say anything. I have the letters from Deacon Turner to prove the affair, and I have read them. I know he was in Dallas to be with you, and I know the two of you were together."

She said he just stared at her, so Pat picked up her bag and walked out of the room. She was literally shaking once she got outside the room. She called me and came directly to my room, where she had broken down and cried. Pat said that was the hardest thing she had ever done, and she was relieved of the pressure.

Pat was in my room for about forty-five minutes when her cell phone started ringing. It was Greg. She didn't want to answer it, and didn't. Their flight was leaving that evening, and she said she did not want to go back on the same flight with him nor did she want to go back anytime soon. I told her I would be in Dallas for another three days for a board meeting. I was on the board of the American Psychologist Association, and we were also meeting in Dallas. My husband went back to Miami the night before. I told her, since we had double beds, if she wanted to stay with me for the next three days just to sort things out, I would be glad to help her do that. She agreed.

Greg continued to call and left several messages, explaining she was going to miss the plane, and they really needed to talk. One message said that if she wasn't going to make their flight, he was not getting on the plane without her. Pat said she didn't care what he did. She just wanted to stay in the room, have room service, and consult with me about what she should do next, and that's exactly what she did. I attended my board meeting, and she stayed in the room over the next three days. Greg continued to call. He missed his plane but eventually got on a plane the next day and went home. He asked her if she had taken another plane and if she was home, but she never responded. She called her kids and said she would be away for a few days.

Pat had a women's conference every year, and it was scheduled within two weeks. She didn't want to return to the church, but we talked about her responsibility to the church and the members. She had been planning this conference all year; she even had out-of-town speakers. I explained to Pat that she needed to talk with Greg and see if they could salvage the marriage. She had to try. I knew many couples that lived separately but together, because of the church and their responsibilities to the ministry. I was not saying this was what Pat should do, but it was something a number of people across this country did. I had counseled a number of first ladies who accepted that life for the sake of the ministry.

Pat explained that she could not do that because it was hard enough living with Greg not allowing her to fully participate in the ministry. "I don't get much benefit from making that kind of sacrifice," she said.

I had to agree with her, but I told her that before she made a decision, she must talk with Greg. She agreed again.

I was very concerned about Pat, so I had her call me as soon as she was home when she had a few moments to spare. What she told me about her day was surprising, but I was proud of the strength she used in her situation.

Pat flew back to Houston on a Monday and went straight to work. She told the kids she would be home that evening, and that was the only way Greg knew she was back in town. Greg called her cell, but she never answered. He called her at work, and when she picked up the phone, he said he wanted to talk with her. She agreed and asked him to meet her at a place near where she worked. He told her he would meet her for lunch.

They met at a café near the government building where Pat worked. The first thing out of Greg's mouth was, "What are you going to do?"

She said, "I don't know. I know I am going to follow through with the women's conference, but after that I am not sure."

"Pat, I promise this will never happen again, just give me another chance. Please don't destroy everything we built."

Pat asked him, "What do you mean?"

"Well, we worked so hard in the ministry, and we have so many responsibilities here. If this got out, it would destroy me. Is that what you want? It would destroy us."

Pat explained, "I don't want to destroy anybody. It looks like you have destroyed yourself.

Greg, if you are willing to get tested for STDs and HIV and agree not to get involved in any more homosexual relationships, I will stay with you. Now, don't misunderstand me, I don't have any intentions of you ever touching me again — I just want to make sure you are not infected. You need to talk with Deacon Turner and tell him it is over, and he needs to find a new church home, because I am not going to look at him every Sunday and neither are you.

Understand this, Greg. I will run for attorney general, and you will be visibly supportive of me running, is that clear?"

"Yes, Pat, I will support you."

"I don't know how long I will be able to keep up this charade, but because of the ministry, I will stay with you. I pray that God will give me the strength to forgive you. I guess what hurts the most is that our life; our marriage is all a lie. You were eager to marry me so you could pastor a church, and I was the cover-up all these years. You treated me terribly at church, not letting me control my own women's department. Greg, all of that will change, is that understood?"

"Yes, Pat, that's understood. Whatever you say. I am just so sorry."

"We are still going to Mary's house for the holiday celebration honoring Jane, so please make plans to go."

"I will, Pat."

Pat talked to me about what happened. She talked about her decision to stay with Greg, if everything checked out with the HIV test and if things changed at the church. She said, "so far, so good. Mary, I am running next term for attorney general and Greg is being very supportive. My career will keep me very busy but at the same time, I am looking forward to a whole new chapter with the ministry at church. This is not going to be an easy road, but I have asked God to give me the strength to do what needs to be done. If it wasn't for our ministry, I know I would divorce Greg. Mary, you have been right all along, this is bigger than Greg and me. God has entrusted us with his people, and I know he will give us what we need to get through this season."

CHAPTER 14

What God Can Do

A Miracle

Pastor Terri and I scheduled the date where I would meet her and her husband in Miami Beach before she left the Pastor's Conference. I wanted to meet them in a neutral place. I thought the first conversation with the three of us might be a little uncomfortable at their church, so we found a great restaurant. They were both on time, and I was relieved to see that Pastor Larry was still very cordial. I started the conversation off with some small talk about the pastors' conference. We all recounted our favorite parts and planned to attend next year.

Right after our order was taken Pastor Larry jumped in and said, "I know what this is about, and Terri and I have really been trying to work this out. I know I have some issues, and we have been fasting and praying." He took a deep breath and took his wife's hand in a gesture of solidarity, and then he looked me in my eyes. "Mary, I've learned and been reminded of a lot of things over the last few months, but one thing I discovered was that having mentors in your life is imperative. As pastors and leaders, we can't be out here by ourselves. Of course, we recognize God is always with us, but it is so important to have a mentor in the ministry. So many of us lose our way, and we don't have anyone that cares enough to pull us to the side." He paused briefly, looking at his wife and looked back at me.

"Bishop T.S. Davis, my Bishop, could see I was struggling, and he approached me at our last conference. He suggested we grab something to eat before we went back to church. I agreed, not having the slightest clue what he was going to say. We went to this restaurant not far from the convention center where we were holding our conference. As we sat down, Bishop said, 'Is everything going okay?' I said, yes. He asked me about the ministry, and I proudly told him it was growing by leaps and bounds. He looked at me intensely then asked, 'How's your family?' I said, They are good. He pointed out that he hadn't seen me in a long time. He said, 'Where have you been?' I told him I had been traveling. I said I had gone to Madrid with a pastor friend of mine. He looked at me, hung his head and said, 'Man, what are you doing?' I told him, Well, I am doing a lot of traveling. He said, 'With your wife?' I said, No, with some other pastors, and named the pastors to let him know these were well-known pastors with megachurches. Bishop bowed his head and began to pray. He started praying about me coming back home. He then said, 'Lord, sanctify your servant for the ministry you have given him. Bring him out from among them who mean him no good.' He prayed so, until I began to cry. I was so convicted. I knew I was mistreating Terri, neglecting my family, turning into someone I really didn't like."

I watched as Terri rubbed her knuckles with her thumb in a soothing gesture. Pastor Larry continued. "I never drank alcohol, and I was with a group that had wine with their meals and sometimes other types of drinks as well. I was never comfortable with that. I hadn't shared anything with Bishop about my family, but he said, 'Go back to your family, love on your wife, and pray that God takes these worldly desires from you.'"

Pastor Larry gave me an imploring look. "Terri can tell you that I haven't been abusive in any way toward her, physically or mentally for over a year. I have asked her for forgiveness, and I have moved back into the bedroom. I don't take any vacations by myself."

Terri said, "Mary, he wanted to tell you that himself. I was eager to call you, but he wanted to look you in the eye and tell you himself so you would know his sincerity."

I was pleasantly surprised. Pastor Larry said he talked with his Bishop, and so did Terri. "We were so appreciative of Jane wanting to help us," Pastor Terri said. Pastor Larry interrupted her in his haste to express himself, and squeezed her hand apologetically. "When Terri explained to me what Jane wrote just before she died, it touched my heart. It made me want to do better." Pastor Terri interrupted. "I knew it would take some time, but things are already so much better."

Pastor Larry gave her an appreciative smile and went on.

"Mary, I got caught up in the hype of having a megachurch, I was able to socialize with other pastors of megachurches, I lost my way, and I forgot what I was supposed to be doing: winning souls. This was all new to me. The church grew so fast, and before we knew it, we had a megachurch with a full-time staff. I started receiving calls from pastors of other ministries wanting to get together with me for lunch and dinner. They were flying all over the country without their wives, and doing whatever they were big enough to do. I just got caught up and wanted to be accepted by other ministers, so I started doing what they were doing. I got to the point where I thought that's what all preachers did once they reached a certain level.

But I discovered along the way that there were upstanding, God-fearing pastors who were not part of that lifestyle. Bishop Davis helped open my eyes, and I discovered not all successful pastors were living in the fast lane. There were those pastors with megachurches whose biggest concern was the ministry and ushering souls to Christ.

Bishop Davis helped put me on the right track, and introduced me to pastors who were living a holy and sanctified life. He said, 'Pastor Larry you can't run with everybody wearing a cross around his neck and carrying a title. In determining the character of a man, it's not what he's wearing, or how big his church is, it's not who he says he is; it is a man doing the right thing when no one is watching because it is the right thing to do.

These men, the bishops and pastors you have associated with, aren't anointed because of their titles. God does the anointing. You have been around a long time, Pastor Larry; you know whether these men are God-anointed. You are an anointed man of God, and you must guard your anointing. Come out from amongst them, as these men could destroy you.'

I thanked Bishop Davis for his counsel. I knew he was right. I had not felt comfortable with these guys since our last trip when they all ordered alcoholic beverages. Every time we ate lunch or dinner, they ordered drinks, and some drank too much. I never ordered wine or any other drink, and I could tell they took offense to that. I told them I had a weak stomach and would get sick, and because we were out of the country I really didn't need to get sick. They just looked at me; I don't think they bought that story.

After talking to Bishop, I didn't care if I never saw any of them again, but I decided to be cordial and just not go out with them. I told Bishop, I just want my family back. Pastor Terri had stopped talking to me, and when I was around the children they would get up and go to another room."

He bowed for a moment, and I saw the weight lift off his shoulders.

"Bishop began to pray for my family and for me," Pastor Larry continued. "From that day to this one, I know I am a new creature in Christ. He has given me a second chance, and I don't take that lightly.

In getting caught up, I forgot what God had given me in Pastor Terri. I was so busy trying to be somebody to those men; I forgot that I was already somebody to those that really mattered. Terri stayed with me through all of my cruelty. I knew she wanted to leave me, but she didn't. She hung in there for the children, for the ministry and I know for me."

In one of our sessions, I asked Terri how she felt about the congregation and about those who were more educated than she was. I looked at Pastor Larry. "Do you think her insecurity in that area is something you might have precipitated?" Pastor Larry said, "I hope not. If I did that through my actions I am terribly sorry.

Was that a problem for her or Pastor Larry? Pastor Larry said, "Terri is the prettiest and sharpest woman at the church, spiritually and naturally. Sometimes the devil plays with your mind and makes you think the grass is greener on the other side. I realized it was only greener because somebody was cultivating it, taking care of it." He looked back at his wife and lifted their clasped hands so that he could place a kiss on the back of hers. "I've started taking care of my wife and my family, and I have asked for forgiveness. I realized Terri is a gift from God and I thank God, and I thank you, Mary, for following Jane's instructions. Terri told me you were a life-saver to her." Pastor Larry said, "Terri was at her wit's end and was thinking unthinkable thoughts, but God sent you, Mary, by way of Jane.

It's as if a light bulb came on in my head. I know the word, I preach it every Sunday, but God had to bring some things to my remembrance through Jane. I almost lost everything: my wife, my children, and my ministry. I almost lost everything because of my ego and getting caught up in this fast-growing ministry; thinking I was larger than life and could do just about anything I wanted. God entrusted me with his people and his church, and I almost lost everything. I thank God for another chance to be the best I can be, to represent Him well."

"Mary, our Bishop has given us some instructions to follow, and we will also work with you," Pastor Terri said.

"I believe you are on the right road; I don't need to give you any instructions. Jane wanted me to direct some attention towards your relationship, and God gave us favor. Pastor Larry, your willingness to change, and your receptivity to your Bishop's and our counseling are producing the desired outcome of healing and reconciliation.

I would be happy to see both of you again in a professional capacity if needed. I'm just a phone call away. But, even more, I'm looking forward to spending time with both of you during the Christmas holidays as we celebrate the life of Jane. If you are able, I would like for both of you to help me with the dinner. I want us to enjoy one another and at the same time, I want us to spend time talking about what Jane meant to each of us. I would like for the two of you to be prepared, and help me get that dialogue going during the Christmas celebration."

The pastors readily agreed. I believe we all were feeling an overwhelming gratefulness toward Jane at that moment and the request she made on their behalf.

CHAPTER 15

Unforgiveness

The ultimate Price

Ron, Jane's husband, called me on a rainy afternoon. He said he was ready to talk to me about Jane's death. The way he sounded frightened me, and I had a feeling he was going to share with me what Jane said he would in her letter. I asked him if I could bring my husband; I didn't want to go by the house alone. He said, "of course." When we got to his house, he hugged both of us with tears in his eyes. Once we were seated in the living room, he said, "I know why Jane killed herself."

I immediately stood up as if that was our cue to immediately leave. I didn't want to hear it. My husband sat me back down, and I just started crying as if I already knew. I just knew it had to be something terrible and bizarre. I was so afraid it was something that could have been fixed, and I wasn't there to help fix it.

Ron sat in the overstuffed chair across from us and began without preamble. "Jane had a daughter when she was fifteen years old, and gave her up for adoption." He rubbed his forehead with his fingers. "She told me about the child early on. When she turned eighteen, we tried to find her. Jane didn't want to spend too much time looking because she was afraid the deeper the investigation was, the more likely the intrusion or interruption would be in her daughter's life. She imagined her daughter having this great life, finishing college and teaching at some great university. Jane was an avid reader and educator; she just knew her daughter would be an educator as well. Jane would talk and imagine all of the lofty goals and wonderful things her daughter was doing. It kept her somewhat content; because it gave her comfort that she did the right thing.

At some point, Jane stopped looking because she didn't want to interfere, but she began to consider the possibly of having grandchildren, and the desire to see those grandchildren outweighed the uneasiness she felt about interfering. She really would want to be a part of their lives. Jane's biggest fear was whether her daughter would accept her after all of that time. Her life was so full, but she never stopped caring about the one daughter she had never met.

Jane and I looked everywhere. We talked to every adoption agency and every hospital in Miami and the surrounding areas. Jane even hired a private investigator and spent thousands of dollars looking for this child. The most difficult part was that Jane didn't have a name; all she had was a date of birth. She did not remember the city or the agency that took her baby. She didn't remember the hospital. We left notes and cards with everyone and anyone, asking if they knew anything regarding the birth of this baby or the adoptive parents.

Jane went through the pregnancy and labor all by herself. Her parents were traveling overseas at the time, and Jane was supposed to be staying with friends while they were in London. Jane's parents were missionaries and traveled away from home for long periods of time. She got involved with a young boy and got pregnant. Jane didn't tell the people she was staying with, and they never knew she was pregnant, since she was very small in stature. No one realized she was pregnant. When it was time for the baby to be born, some friends of the boy took her to a nearby town. By the time we talked about it, Jane had blocked out the whereabouts of the little town."

I could see Ron was struggling to get the story out, but I didn't know if my hug would strengthen or break him, so I remained where I was. Ron explained that they got a call from an adoption agency right in Miami, who had information about the family who adopted a little girl at the same time Jane put hers up for adoption. There were quite a few similarities between what Jane could remember and what the family placed in the open records. The agency had an address and a phone number. Jane called the number, but it was no longer in service. They were given an address but soon discovered the family no longer lived there. The address was located in a public housing project in one of the worst areas in Miami; it was a high-rise building with security bars all the way to the top. Jane had never been in this area of town. They did find people who knew the couple and the daughter. Jane and Ron were told the couple moved to Iowa, but no one knew where the daughter moved. They were adamant about the daughter not moving to Iowa with the couple.

In Jane's letter to Ron, she wrote, "How do you deal with the guilt and the shame? Does the pain in the bottom of your stomach ever go away? Who do you talk to? Nobody can help me with this. I did it, and I can't fix it. Should I have tried harder to find her? I never should have stopped looking for her. When we make this kind of mistake, who do we turn to? I often wonder if I should have turned to my parents. It would have been hard to see their disappointment, but they wouldn't have thrown my baby away. Why did I think I couldn't go to my parents? Did they give any indication they would disown me or give the baby away? Abortion was out of the question for them, and it was out of the question for me. My parents loved me, and they wouldn't have given my baby away."

Jane was dealing with this constant pain. The guilt and the shame were eating at her and on top of all of that, she was a first lady of a thirty-thousand-member congregation with all of the stress and pressure that went along with the title.

Ron said that the week before the first Sunday in June—the Sunday Jane took her life—she received a letter from one of the sources where they had left the information regarding her daughter. The letter basically said that the young lady you had been looking for was named Iris. Iris was twenty-six years old and had struggled with a heroin addiction for about two years. She'd died of an overdose last year in Miami. The close of the letter said, "We are sorry for your loss."

"This letter was more than Jane could take," Ron said. "It was so hard for her to forgive herself for giving her daughter away. She believed her daughter's life would have been so different if she hadn't been given away. Jane blamed herself for the death of her daughter, and she just could not live with that thought."

The pain of that statement struck me so hard that all I could do was cry for my friend and what she went through. I wanted to cry at the injustice of it all. She had so many people who loved her, so many friends, and her friends, like her, also had multiple issues in addition to being the first lady of the church. As a friend, I failed.

As I continued to think about Jane, we all failed. We failed to step outside of ourselves and help those who were hurting around us. We must be more sensitive to those we love and to those we see every week in our churches. We need to be more sensitive to our members. We know when people are hurting; we sense it, and we see it, and we have to reach out more when we see those in need. When Jane wanted to meet with me for lunch, it seemed a little unusual how she approached me. We have to pay attention to those around us, even our members.

We have to listen attentively to those who are taking the time to reach out to their pastors, particularly to those who seldom reach out and share. We must hear the silent pleas for help and act on them.

I can't begin to understand not forgiving yourself to the point of not wanting to live. It is just as bad when you choose not to forgive another person. When we choose not to forgive another human being for what they have done to you, it's not hurting the person; we're hurting ourselves. It's like what Jane did; you are feeding yourself the poison. When someone hurts you, it's hard to forgive. You want to forgive, you say you forgive, but in the back of your mind, you really haven't forgiven. It will fester and become toxic. This is something you ask God to take away. It's too hard to do alone.

As I thought about Jane and how I missed the signs, as a pastor's wife, I considered how awesome the responsibility, to be sensitive to the needs of those you serve and love. It's interesting how people see the glamour and think this is a great life. It is a great life, but not for the reasons people think. It's a life of service, assisting and meeting the needs of others, and for this, it is a great life.

For Jane, the ultimate price for unforgiveness was the loss of her life. Although Jane and I were close friends, unforgiveness imprisoned her; it kept her from becoming free. It prevented Jane from sharing with me. I know she wanted to and tried to reach out to me on several different occasions, but I didn't see it at the time.

Unforgiveness drains the joy from living; it paralyzes the one who refuses to forgive, and it impairs your judgment. I believe this is what happened to Jane.

Unforgiveness forecloses on the Grace of God because God says that unless we forgive, our sins remain.

Unforgiveness is an act where you choose to play God, but God says, "Vengeance is mine."

Jane knew better than me that this is a daily walk, and we must live life God's way.

Jane refused to do it God's way, but for the sake of my immediate family and church family I must forgive myself for not being there for my friend or hearing her cries, and I will with God's help.

Before we left Ron's house that evening, I stood before him and asked his forgiveness for not being sensitive to Jane's call for help. He shook his head, saying that there was nothing to apologize for because, ultimately, Jane chose the path she took. "But if you need to hear it Mary, I forgive you, and I will continue to seek God to help me forgive myself," he said, before pulling me into a hug that helped to soothe some of the pain, I think, for both of us.

Jane refused to do it God's way.

CHAPTER 16

In Jane's Honor

Embrace the Present

It was that special time of the year. Even though the changing of the seasons wasn't as pronounced in Miami as it was in Kansas City or South Bend, there was something about Christmas time; it was a wonderful time of the year no matter where you lived.

I had decided to invite clients and friends who were friends of Jane Steinbeck to my home to celebrate Jane's life and her many contributions. I thought long and hard about my invitation list. I invited pastors Larry and Terri Jones, pastors Gregory and Patricia Harris, pastors Alonzo and Plessey Humphrey, and Elona Braggs. These were dear friends of Jane's, and there was no question as to whether or not I would invite them. They just had to be there. Of course, Jane's husband, Ron, Ron Jr., Stacy, Madeline, Bryan, and all the grandchildren were invited. They all came, and Ron thanked me for honoring Jane.

Ron had been at the receiving end of so many people's pain and anger regarding Jane. So many saw her act as a cop-out, but no one understood the struggle she endured and sacrifice she made day after day. Ron was tired of people not appreciating Jane's life. Everyone was upset with how Jane died, and they really resented the fact that she took her own life. But they had no clue. All they saw were her titles, prestige, and opulence, but they had no understanding of what those things cost or the toll they took. No one was aware of the late night counseling, or the urgent and unrelenting prompting of the Holy Ghost to pray for a single individual or family way before the sun came up. There was no pomp and circumstance when she walked into a homeless shelter and handed out gift bags to children who had forgotten the meaning of Christmas. There were no cameras rolling while she led a person to the Lord who had run from Him so long that he accepted Jesus into his heart mere seconds before his soul was delivered into His hands. They also weren't in the room the week before the first Sunday in June, when Jane opened the letter that would tip her world off its axis.

I thought about what I was trying to accomplish: to remember someone who cared deeply for all of us, and for us to really spend some relaxed social time together, honoring her memory. Jane thought we were all worth saving. The closer we came to the party, the happier I was that I'd chosen the

Christmas season. It was such a miraculous and beautiful time of the year, even in Miami. For me, Christmas always spoke of the possibility of new beginnings. I think it was the overwhelming sense of love that filled the air.

Everyone I invited to the holiday party to celebrate Jane's life agreed to come – even Elona Braggs. She was coming to the United States just for this holiday dinner. I was so excited and thankful that she thought so much of Jane. I invited a few members from Jane's church that were close to me, including Jane's assistant, Lisa, and her husband. I invited about twenty-five people, and prepared a sit-down dinner. I wanted this evening to be a celebration.

Elona, Patricia, Terri and Plessey had all agreed to meet me for brunch the morning after our dinner. We wanted to talk intimately between just the five of us about our journey with, and because of, Jane.

Although I knew what I wanted the conversation to center around during the celebratory dinner, I hadn't given much thought to how specific personal conversations would go. I prepared an opening statement about Jane and her life, and decided I would then open it up to anyone who wanted to share about themselves and Jane. I wanted to keep it informal. Those who wanted to say something would be permitted. However, it would not be mandatory. I just wanted people that loved Jane to be together.

The time was quickly approaching, and I had everything prepared. The dinner was being catered with festive holiday food: honey baked ham and turkey with all the trimmings. Some young ladies from my church had asked to be servers at the meal when they learned I was having a Christmas party. I was very thankful they volunteered. I also had young men outside, parking the cars, because there was not a lot of parking space around my house, and I didn't want my guests to have to walk far. Everything was working out perfectly.

The first to arrive at my house were Pastors Larry and Terri Jones. They arrived early because Pastor Terri wanted to help. I was so appreciative that I could barely contain myself. She helped with the seating chart, and arranged my fresh flowers. She had such a great eye for things like that.

I didn't have a set program for the evening. I wanted us to have fellowship together, enjoy the food and, at some point during the evening, we would pay tribute to Jane and give everybody an opportunity to share.

It seemed as if everyone else began arriving close to the same time. Elona Braggs and a security person walked in. On the porch behind her were pastor Greg and his wife, Patricia Harris. Plessey Humphrey came by herself, and I was really glad to see her.

Ron, Ron. Jr., Stacy, Madeline (accompanied by a young woman I assumed was her friend), Bryan, and the grandchildren were the last to arrive. All of my invited guests came except Plessey's husband, Alonzo.

The house was decorated beautifully. We had all these great sitting areas, and everybody made themselves at home.

We started the sit-down dinner about forty-five minutes after everybody arrived. The food looked wonderful, and everybody enjoyed it. Towards the end of the dinner, I stood up and said, "We are all here because of Jane Steinbeck. She touched each one of our lives in a special way. We all knew her from different walks of life. I would like to start by sharing my connection to Jane." I took a deep breath and began.

"I knew Jane for over twenty-five years. We met overseas. My husband and I do a lot of missionary work in Africa and other parts of the world. We have always focused on children. We attended the dedication of an orphanage in Haiti, and Jane and Ron were there.

"There were about fifty people in attendance; fifteen of us were from the United States. Jane and I clicked right away. When we discovered we were both from Florida, we became attached at the hip." There was easy laughter around the table. "We were friends ever since. I am from a more conservative church – Presbyterian – and Jane had a Pentecostal background, but we just seemed to hit it off from the very first time we met. As most of you know, Jane doesn't meet any strangers. I have never shared this with anyone but, ten years ago, I was going through a very difficult time, trying to balance my career and being first lady at the church. I was really torn over what I should be doing. Jane sat me down and said, 'Mary, your ministry is important at the church. Your direction is needed within your department of women and helping those women in need. Your ministry at your office is also important, because everyone you see needs help.' She told me I had 'a gift from God to help those in the church and to help those outside the church.' I never thought of those I helped outside the church as my ministry until Jane made me see it. She told me I had the responsibility of helping those that were hurting. There was no reason to be torn between assignments because they were both equally my assignments. Jane went on to say that there was truly only one assignment – to help the lost, the hurting, the unlovable, the downtrodden, those who couldn't see their way, and those who needed to know that there was a better way and a better life. She told me my assignment was bigger than the church; my assignment extended to God's people from all walks of life, whether they were Presbyterian, Baptist, Pentecostal or Agnostic. I never looked at my work in this way. Jane helped me to see that what I was doing was valuable in my walk with Christ. I will forever be in her debt. We talked almost every day but, unfortunately, I couldn't help her. She reached out to all of us, and deposited something in all of our lives, and none of us could help her.

"I wanted all of us to be together, because we have a special bond with each other, and that's Jane's love." I paused. "I'm finished."

I sat down and was comforted by my husband's hand covering mine and giving me a gentle squeeze. I smiled at him, and then looked over at Jake and received a small smile of comfort from him as well. I took a deep, cleansing breath, and looked over to Pastor Terri as she stood.

"I just wanted to say – I am celebrating Jane's life because she poured so much into mine," Pastor Terri said abruptly. "I think Jane was the only person I talked to about what was going on in my home. She prayed for me. We were prayer partners and prayed every week together, just the two of us. She had thirty thousand members in her congregation, and she took time to pray for me and I prayed for her. I never knew what was troubling Jane, but I knew something was there, and I prayed. We prayed every week, and we talked to each other during that time. She wanted to know how my children were and if things were getting better. She cared about me, and I knew it. She will always be special to me. I will never forget the love she had for our family. Jane saved my life and my husband's life; she saved our marriage and our ministry, and I will be eternally grateful." With tears in her eyes, Terri sat down and her husband embraced her. Not more than a couple of seconds went by before Elona Braggs stood up.

"Most of you know me," said Elona Braggs. "I am from London, England. I travel back and forth ministering in the United States. Jane and I met in Africa about twenty years ago, and we have been friends ever since that time. We always spent time together when I was in the United States, even if it was just to share a cup of coffee at the airport. We did that once. I was leaving, and Jane said she would meet me at the airport for coffee, and she did. She said, 'I just wanted to give you a big hug and let you know God has not forgotten you.'" Visibly struggling to keep from losing her composure, Elona bit her bottom lip as she took in several deep breaths and expelled them as slowly as she could. Still, a few tears escaped, and she wiped them away. "Please forgive me for crying, but who does that? Who goes that far out of their way? She didn't live close to the airport – she lived on the other side of town – but she wanted me to know God had not forgotten me. I have ministered all over the world, even before kings and queens. I have been in places I have only dreamed about. God has given me His unmerited favor to succeed beyond my wildest dreams in ministry, which I love with every breath I take." Her accent became even stronger with her passionate speech. "And someone travels across the city to see me at the airport to tell me – me – that God has not forgotten me. This woman of God touched my heart on more than one occasion. She could have cared less about where I had been and to whom I had ministered; she just wanted me to know that God had not forgotten me. Jane knew my struggle and my battle with depression, and she always had an uplifting word for me. No matter how many words I had for someone else, she always had a word for me." Elona paused. "Thank you so much for inviting me to this special occasion. Jane was special. She was unique, and she cared so much for others. I know my life is more valuable for having known her. I love you all."

I cleared my throat. "Before we continue – as most of you know, right before Jane took her life, she wrote a letter concerning each of you." I looked around the table, letting my eyes linger on those she'd singled out in her letter. "She wanted me to check on each of you. She was thinking about you during her last hours on earth. She asked me to help you in any way I could. She named each one of you, one by one. I often think about the awesome responsibility she gave me. In the beginning, I was intimidated by the assignment. I wondered how I would touch each one of your lives." I paused, shaking my head at what some would call irony, but what I knew for a fact: this was just how God worked. "You have no idea how each of you have ministered to me. There is one thing I discovered during this journey – that each one of you love the Lord, and that's why Jane loved you so much. She knew that. She knew about the anointing on each of your lives and how you minister on a daily basis to those in your congregations. She knew it was important that if you needed help, you should get it, because God had put this awesome responsibility in your hands to care for His People. Thank you so much for coming. Would anyone else like to share this evening?"

"I would like to say something. My name is Plessey Humphrey," Plessey said, standing. "I didn't know Jane; I just feel like I knew her. All of you are so rich because you knew her. Thank you for allowing me to be a part of your celebration of Jane's life. Because of Jane, I was able to get help as well. I thank my friend Elona Braggs for coming into my life and giving me this opportunity. My journey in this maze is nowhere near over, but God has given me friends like you, and a stronger faith to just sit still and let him fight my battle.

"For I am confident of this very thing, that He who began a good work in you will perfect it until the day of Christ Jesus. Philippians 1:6."

Everybody hugged Plessey.

"Jane would have wanted you to be a part of this group," I said, giving her what I knew was a watery smile.

I looked around the room. "Well, is there anyone else? What about you, Patricia?"

Patricia stood and said she was really happy to be at the celebration. She began to cry and said,

"I thank God for Jane and for Mary, my new friend. I want to ask each of you to continue to pray for us. I am having a serious problem with forgiveness. I know I have to forgive, but please pray for us."

Greg got up and put his arms around his wife and said,

"We are taking it one day at a time."

"We will continue to pray for you, Patricia. For both of you, Greg," I said. I turned to Jane's husband. "Ron, would you like to say anything? You don't have to."

He nodded his head and stood slowly. He looked as though he had aged five years over the last twenty-two months, but tonight there was a light in his eyes I hadn't seen for a long time.

"Well, I want to thank all of you for coming to celebrate my wife's life. This means so much to our family. All of you knew Jane, and the kind of life she lived. We carried a secret for over 20 years, and I prayed she would mentally move on and forgive herself for what happened. I recently told Mary about it, but I would like to share it with all of you."

He cleared his throat and continued. "She really tried to forgive herself, but she just couldn't. It lets us know that even the best of us can be tricked by the devil. Jane was such a believer and had so much faith. Being unforgiving is a deadly evil that can ultimately kill. Patricia, I don't know what you are going through, but you must forgive; sometimes our life depends on it. Jane loved all of you and wanted you to be whole." Then he turned to me. "Mary, you have been such an anchor for our family and for Jane. Jane wanted to talk with you, and she could have tried harder but she chose not to. She made this decision all by herself. The guilt was eating her up, and she couldn't bear it. I did all I knew how to do but, Mary, I should have called you. My concern was that this was so personal to Jane; I didn't feel comfortable in making that call. If I had known this was a life-threatening event, I would not have hesitated." His daughter Madeline, who was sitting in the chair next to him, took his hand. He smiled down at her and seemed to receive strength from her touch.

"We have to be sensitive to one another, and when we see our brother or our sister hurting, because we are a part of the Body of Christ, we need to inquire and let them know we are there if they need us. I have found through this tragedy in our family that we have to be more proactive. If our heart is in the right place when we reach out, our help will be accepted. We have to do our part, and let God do the rest. Our hearts are heavy today because I have lost my wife, and my children have lost their mother. I know you have lost her as well. In honoring Jane's life, one of the most important things we can do is love one another and make sure we are free from any unforgiveness.

"As leaders, it is so important that we live a life before our people that they can emulate – a life that honors God. Thank you again for coming. Thank you, Mary."

"Thank you, Ron," I said. "I want to thank everyone for coming. I want to thank this family for allowing us to celebrate Jane's life. She poured some of herself into all of us. I would like for this to be an annual celebration. It will give us an opportunity to see one another and stay in touch. I know if we all go to the pastors' conference in Dallas, we will see each other during that week, but this – this will be our special time.

"God placed us together through Jane, and it would be great if we could continue that relationship. We have so much in common.

"As a first lady in ministry, I have discovered the rewards are so much greater than the ups and downs we experience. We have this wonderful opportunity to touch lives and to be a part of so many families. God has given us this wonderful assurance:

'For I reckon that the sufferings of this present time are not worthy to be compared with the glory which shall be revealed in us. Romans 8:18'.

"We have to continue our work; we have an awesome responsibility to the Body of Christ. No matter what it looks like, as my friend Evangelist Coaster said in a revival, 'we must have strong faith to have a strong finish.' We all know this is a faith walk, with all of our imperfections, but God still loves us."

Greg broke down at that moment, crying, and looked to his wife Pat. He took her hand, barely able to get the words out and said,

"Please forgive me, Pat."

Pat looked at him and then looked at all of us and said,

"Please pray for me. I just need your prayers."

Pastor Larry walked over to Pastor Greg and placed a hand on his shoulder and told him,

"You have to remember that God can do anything but fail. Hold on to that, and don't stop praying! I am where I am today because of prayer. I talked to my Bishop, I talked to Mary, and they really helped, but nothing helped like me getting on my knees crying out to God and asking for His help."

Pastor Larry continued. "The Bible says in *Matthew 6:6, But thou, when thou prayest, enter into thy closet, and when thou hast shut thy door, pray to thy father which is in secret: and thy Father which seeth in secret shall reward thee openly.* Greg, some things we can't share with anybody but God, and we have to believe that we will receive an answer from Him and that He will bring us out all right. Greg, you have to believe that."

Pastor Greg, talking softly to Pastor Larry, said,

"Pastor Larry, I need your help. I want to change my life. I am going to need some continued professional help, and Mary has agreed to work with me. I am so afraid Pat is not going to forgive me, and she may leave me."

Pastor Larry quickly said,

"Greg, she has to forgive you, not for you but for herself. She will not make it in the ministry if she doesn't forgive. She's not going to make it in her job if she doesn't forgive you. Unforgivingness is like a cancer: if you hold onto it, it will kill you." Pastor Larry continued to minister to Greg as Pastor Terri walked over to Pat and grabbed her and just held her.

Pat began to cry and share with Terri.

"It is just so hard for me to forgive. I want to – God knows I want to – but every time I think about our marriage and the years I spent with this man which are based on a lie…it's just hard."

Pastor Terri said,

"Pat, I know it's hard. Larry physically abused me for ten years. Sometimes I couldn't get out of bed, but God delivered him and gave me the strength to forgive him and to love him again. If God can do that for me, I know He can do this for you." Pat sniffed into the tissue Terri had handed her.

"Terri, just continue to pray for me." Terri kept one arm around Pat and squeezed her.

"I will continue to pray for you, but you must have a made-up mind to want to do the right thing. If Jane has taught us anything, she taught us we must forgive to have a victorious life. Pat, think about Jane. She needed us, and we were not there for her, but we are here for you, and we are not going anywhere. We will be here for you and for Greg. We want you to make it and, if it's God's will, you *will* make it and become a family again."

The evening ended with a lot of hugging and exchanging of phone numbers and addresses. Jane would have been so happy to see all of us together. We all wanted to continue this celebration in the coming years.

Before everyone left, I asked Ron to introduce us to the quiet woman that had accompanied the Steinbeck family. I didn't want to appear rude, and if they had invited her to come, she must have been pretty close to the family. With tears in his eyes, he said,

"I wanted to share with all of you what Jane and I had been going through." Ron began to share the story of Jane being pregnant at 15, giving her daughter up for adoption, and later spending several years looking for her daughter. He told everyone of the painful search he and Jane went through for several years. He explained that Jane received word that her daughter had died of a drug overdose. Jane could not live with the fact she had given her daughter up for adoption, with the hopes of a better life.

"What we recently discovered," Ron painfully went on to say, "Was that the young lady who died of an overdose was not Jane's daughter," as he wiped away the tears.

There was complete silence.

Ron continued, "One of the adoption agencies we had been working with called me two months ago, and said there was a young lady looking for her mother. There was a thorough investigation and they discovered that she, Carla – not the other woman – was Jane's daughter." As I looked at the women in wide-eyed astonishment, the similarities became clear. She even favored Madeline, Jane's youngest daughter.

"I want to introduce all of you to Carla, Jane's daughter." Ron went on. "Carla is a professor at Case Western Reserve University in Cleveland, Ohio. She had been looking for her mother for several years."

The young woman spoke up, looking at Ron for permission. "May I say something?"

"Of course," he said, nodding.

She looked around the room at us, and I noticed she also had Jane's warm eyes. My heart gave a funny leap in my chest.

"My name is Carla Slater. I had been looking for my mother for many years. I had wonderful adoptive parents who loved me very much, and gave me a great education and a wonderful Christian home. After listening to each of you and listening to Ron as he shared with me what my mother was like, I am so proud to be her daughter. I know she loved me more than life itself. She also loved each and every one of you," she said, smiling at each person individually. Then she looked at me. "Mary, thank you for sharing how my mother felt about her friends that were first ladies and the responsibility and sometimes the burdens she had to bear. Thank you for letting her into your heart and your life." She took a deep breath and addressed the room as a whole.

"Unforgiveness can trap the best of us. Don't let forgiving yourself, or anyone else for that matter, destroy your life. As I listened to Pat and Greg, I know that whatever price has to be paid to forgive one another, it has to be paid. Your lives may depend on it. Thank you all for loving my mother enough to make her sacrifice count."

Carla turned and hugged Ron, and we couldn't help but show her comfort and love by embracing her in our arms as well, first as a group then individually.

In a way, it was as though Jane had graced us with her presence in this woman, and we were ever so grateful for the gifts of life she hoped we could celebrate. Carla was a gift from God.

"Thank you for loving my mother."

CHAPTER 17

When Is The First Lady Ever First?

There is an Answer

The celebration dinner was a wonderful way to pay tribute to Jane. I am meeting Elona, Patricia, Plessey and Terri for brunch this morning. I wanted all of us to meet Tuesday, the day after the celebratory dinner, just the five of us. I wasn't sure when we would all be together again. Although we planned to be together next year, the five of us needed some time together.

Tuesday morning everyone had arrived. I chose Alexis Café in Miami for brunch. This high end, quaint restaurant had no menus. If you go to Alexis' for dinner, you are asks about your preferences and the chef prepares a personalized six course meal based on your likes and dislikes. The service and food was excellent. I had reserved this room several days in advance and sat with one of the chefs to come up with a wonderful brunch.

Alexis Café had ten private rooms with an open sitting area when you first walk in. I specifically chose a small private room that faced the ocean. There was a small patio connected to the room, with plush lounging chairs. A continual breeze from the ocean kept everyone cool while they milled around talking about what a wonderful time we had at the celebratory dinner, honoring Jane. There was a lot of discussion about Carla, Jane's daughter and how much she looked like Jane.

The Brunch was set up as a buffet in our private dining room. We came inside and selected our food from the wide array of mouth-watering dishes. Everyone talked about the brunch being such a lovely idea. There was one large round table where we all sat together. The food and its presentation were amazing.

There was a lot of small talk about the different plans scheduled for the next year. Elona talked about the possibility of moving to the States because she spends more time here than at home. Patricia was gearing up for the election for the Office of Attorney General of Texas. She was pleased with her husband's show of support. Plessey had an upcoming women's conference and Elona had agreed to be her keynote speaker. Terri was busy with their church and she and Pastor Larry were in the process of purchasing land to establish a center for restoring leaders.

We had finished eating and Elona said, "Mary we have dined sufficiently and we have had great fellowship but why am I thinking there is more to this brunch than food and fellowship?" "Well Elona, there is. I have given a lot of thought about first ladies and I wanted to share some things with just the four of you. When we say First Lady, we could be talking about the mayor's wife, the governor's wife or even Michelle Obama. The title encompasses everything we do and it is both impressive and daunting.

I had the pleasure of getting to know each one of you on a professional basis as well as on a personal level. You are my friends. We all have Jane and her desire to want to help first ladies, in common.

I want to try to answer a question Jane posed to me several years ago, and again in her last letter to me; although she asked it in jest, she said, '*When is the first lady ever first?*' I pulled from my experiences with not only you ladies but from my thirty years of work experience, and my working knowledge as a Pastor's wife for over twenty-five years. I want to share my answer with you but first I want to preface this answer with some of the things we, as first ladies are faced with on a regular basis."

I looked around the table, watching some of the women shift in their seats and begin to focus intently on my words.

"Sometimes, members look toward the pulpit on a Sunday or on the dais during a banquet and see the first lady reserved and very quiet, not saying much at all to anybody. She does not appear to be aloof, but just very protective because she has heard so much and seen so much; she is reluctant to open up to anyone."

I watched some of the women nod as I spoke the next few words.

"People talk about her, talk about her husband, and talk about her children. Members actually pick up the phone wanting the first lady to be aware of what's going on behind her back, thinking they are doing her a service. There are times when the first lady gets overwhelmed to the point that she just shuts down. She's reluctant to answer the phone because her so-called 'member friends' call to give her a blow-by-blow of what's being said and by whom," to which provoked a rousing simultaneous 'AMEN' from Plessey and Terri who then stared at one another and broke out in laughter.

"The First Lady is always the first responder when it comes to the Pastor; she is the first one on her feet when he's preaching. However, as shared with me, this Sunday is different. This Sunday the First Lady was sitting down, and the Pastor was preaching harder than ever before. Everybody was standing but her. Everyone is wondering why the First Lady was not standing; her hands were folded, and she was looking at the floor with a blank stare.

We have no idea what it took for her to get there this Sunday morning. We weren't there when the man preaching his heart out cussed her out before they left home, and she just doesn't have the strength to pretend this Sunday."

Both Terri and Patricia bowed their heads as if they were lost in thought.

"There are many who think the first lady's life is all glamorous; you dress up, you put on wonderful hats and matching shoes, you walk into the sanctuary and all eyes are on you. Well, you pay a price for this journey.

I wouldn't describe it as all glamorous; it is a humbling experience to be this closely and personally involved in ministry."

I looked at Elona when I felt her grab my hand and squeeze it. Although she was not married I could feel her understanding from the brief touch. I took a deep breath and continued.

"It is an awesome responsibility to be entrusted with the oversight and the spiritual care of people. To fulfill this responsibility, you have to recognize you are accountable to God. You are required to be disciplined, faithful, and you must have integrity. Further, to fulfill this responsibility, you must not only love God you must love God's people.

After watching each of you; talking to you, counseling you, being a part of your ministry, sharing your ups and downs; without a shadow of a doubt, I know you love God and you love God's people."

I slowly scanned the table, making sure to meet each person's eyes.

In a very quiet voice I said, "I know Jane loved God and she loved God's people."

It seemed to take an extraordinary amount of willpower to speak around the lump forming in my throat, but after a small pause I composed myself enough to keep speaking.

"But she was deeply wounded and never recovered. She loved on the people, she ministered to the lost, she prayed for the sick, loved on the mothers and the youth with a gaping, festering wound in her heart for several years. To me, she hid it well because her ministry was a gift from God and as we all know, a gift from God is without repentance. I wish I had known that Jane had plunged so deep into the abyss of grief and guilt that she lost her ability to care for herself. I now see how hard it must have been for her to come back, from where she was, on her own."

I didn't even try to stop the tears this time, but I let my indignation at the avoidable loss of my friend spur me on.

"Her wound became fatal because she failed to seek healing from the same God to which she constantly directed others. Being on the 'front line' of God's army, there are more opportunities for us to be wounded. God through His Word and our relationship with Him, has taught us how to heal ourselves, surrender to Him for restoration or take preventative measures by, '*putting on the whole armor of God that ye may be able to stand against the wiles of the devil*'. Ephesians 6:11."

I swiped at my tear-streaked cheeks and took a cleansing breath. This was a challenge I needed them to enlist in with me; for their sakes and for the sake of allowing Jane's death to teach us how to avoid yet another pitfall.

"What I fear we are overlooking is our own soul's fragility when we restrict the flow of God's healing to any part of our life. It's like cutting off the blood flow to a part of our body. Over time it will wither and die.

Somewhere Jane lost her way. Somewhere she forgot that she was an intricate part of the Body of Christ. She had access to an eternal lifeline, which would have fed her the hope she needed to survive; the hope she needed to reclaim her joy; the hope she spoke into all of our lives. Jane also forgot she had a lifeline to us. We loved her and she needed us, but her unwillingness to open up to us and be ministered to as she ministered to us, prevented her from receiving her much needed healing. We as first ladies are pretty resilient, but we are only as strong as our ability to surrender our weaknesses over to God. When Jane stopped seeking healing from God and wouldn't open up to receive help from us, she cut her lifelines.

I can't tell you how important I think it is that we don't forget that the devil comes to steal, kill and destroy. It doesn't all happen at once, but it works like a slow acting poison that moves through the body, killing everything in its wake.

He killed Jane's hope; he stole her joy and destroyed her life, but it could have been avoided if she only followed the advice you said she gave you Patricia." I looked at Patricia and she looked back at me in confusion, but as I continued I could see comprehension form in her eyes.

"That was for you to forgive, because without it you are gradually restricting God's healing love to flow through each and every part of your life." I looked around the table again because she was not alone in this.

"This, I believe was her wonderful advice for all of us, not just to forgive those that hurt us, but to forgive ourselves."

The slow nods and thoughtful expressions around the table only confirmed the need for this time of sharing and fellowship and I finally felt the weight that God had placed on my heart regarding this subject and these women begin to lift.

"You know, Mary, everything you have said so far has resounded in me, so I know it was no one but God who ordained this time and gave you this word for us. I know I'm not only speaking for myself when I say Thank you for allowing yourself to be used in such a powerful way," Elona said, while she looked at the rest of the women who nodded or stated their agreement.

Then her piercing blue eyes held mine. "I also know that you have been wrestling with your own guilt for not noticing what was going on with Jane. You too need to forgive yourself because you have been allowing the enemy to condemn you for things you are not guilty of. You are going to have to let that go." I nodded my head, unable to speak around the emotion clogging my throat. She got up and moved closer to embrace me. "I know God has been ministering to you even as he has been pouring into you for us." She spoke softly in my ear. "He started the healing process through Jane, but she was only able to plant the seed. We will see it grow."

At these words something released inside me. Maybe it was the last reservation of doubt or the guilt I was holding onto, but I felt like weeping for joy in what I felt was just imparted in me. I hugged her tighter while I cried and slowly felt more arms wrap around us. When I finally lifted my head we were one group embracing each other. I couldn't help the watery laugh that came to my lips and soon we were all full of teary laughter.

After a much needed trip to the ladies room to restore our makeup we went back to the room and I was happy to see that the special desserts and coffees I had ordered for everyone had been laid out on the table.

I'd just taken the last bite of my deep dark chocolate soufflé when Terri spoke. "So you started to tell us about the question Jane asked, *'When is the first lady ever first?'* I for one would like to know the answer to that question".

"Me too because honestly, sometimes it seems just the opposite." Plessey commented.

I pushed my plate away, feeling the energy in the room shift. I cleared my throat before I began, seeing the looks of expectation on their faces.

"When is the first lady ever first? I used to think, maybe never, but I thought about what each of you do everyday as the first lady and you have shared some stories with me that you have allowed me to share today.

God has placed you in a position of confidence with members and friends. They share their most intimate problems with you first. You have the opportunity to see lives changed, families reunited, and witness those who felt they had no way out, find a way through God. You have an opportunity to be exposed to all that God has to offer when a life is changed; when someone becomes a new creature in Christ.

God has given you favor and discernment to know when a young girl is wrestling with whether or not to keep a baby or abort the child conceived out of wedlock. Your counsel may save a life.

God has placed you in the hearts of the mothers and they develop a bond with you simply because of the attention given and visits made, especially in those closing days when they confide in you before they make their transition. You have the privilege of giving them the assurance that their faith was not in vain. When the first lady takes the time to love on the mothers who are sometimes forgotten, all of you know, the joy that brings. Sometimes, we just have to show up!

You are an integral part of the lives of your youth and the high school graduates as they make their choices of college and career. You, as first ladies, have the opportunity to impart wisdom and counsel at the most critical stage in their lives, letting them know it isn't about the type of career or job they plan to acquire. It is the integrity, passion, and diligence in striving to do something with their lives. You have gifted them with the knowledge of how to be the best they can be, and the understanding of the fact that they may have to be better than that, and that's when God takes them to the next level.

The first lady makes an impression when she sees one of the mothers, who just came out of service, waiting at the bus stop in front of the church and she takes the opportunity to reach out to the mother, not only offering her a ride, but making sure she never has to sit at the bus stop after church again. Right at that moment, the first lady has touched a life and made a lasting impression.

At the end of the day, as a first lady, you know better than anyone, what it takes for you and your husband to develop mutual respect; for you to fulfill your responsibility of being a companion and for him to fulfill his responsibility of providing for you and protecting you. When that's accomplished the first lady can walk in her place of influence alongside her husband, and they can be the leaders God has chosen to serve and lead the people."

I glanced down at my lap as I considered all of the things these women had gone through and they were still standing on their faith, fully equipped to minister and willing to give their life to His cause.

I slowly stood, honored to be in the presence of such powerful women of God, and said,

"THE FIRST LADY *IS FIRST WHEN SHE FULFILLS HER CALLING TO BE A WOUNDED HEALER, AN INSTRUMENT IN THE HANDS OF GOD FOR HEALING AND REDEMPTION. SHE'S FIRST WHEN SHE IS DOING WHAT GOD CALLED HER TO DO".*

CHAPTER 18

Holiday Celebration

Nothing Stays the Same

It's been three years since we were all together to honor Jane. I am preparing for what I really wanted to be an Annual Christmas party in Jane's honor. We have had a difficult time getting back together. It's hard to gather a group of busy people. My husband and I looked forward to this time of sharing with our friends. I used to call them Jane's friends, but these are truly our friends, and we have enjoyed their fellowship through the years. Jane knew what each of us needed. Although she did not specifically call me out, she knew I needed some guidance as well.

We are looking forward to seeing Pastors Larry and Terri Jones, who have added some exciting new ministries to what they are already doing in Miami. Their church has grown to be the largest church in Miami Beach. Their television ministry includes a talk show focused on forgiveness and reconciliation. It is powerful, and many leaders and viewers have been helped through this ministry. This family shares their story of how God delivered them, and they never fail to mention Jane and how she was an integral part of their deliverance. These Pastors have established a facility called the City of Restoration that sits on 300 acres of land in Mississippi, and is designed to meet the needs of hurting leaders. This includes those leaders who are alcohol and drug dependent. There is a place for leaders who are just burned out and need a place to be spiritually restored.

They also established a facility at the City of Restoration that provides temporary housing for abused first ladies and other female leaders and their children. The facility is named JANE'S Healing Center, known as JANE'S. There is a large group of volunteers at JANE'S who are there to aid the professional staff and gain experience in this area of ministry. I am honored to be a part of their ministry, and I have referred a number of leaders to this facility.

Evangelist Elona Bragg's ministry has excelled into other countries. She is still single, but believing God for her husband. The ministry keeps her very busy but she, like me, has referred many people to JANE'S. She grew very close to Pastor Larry and Terri when she spent several weeks at JANE'S and the City of Restoration, not only ministering but being ministered to. Since Elona usually takes a four-week holiday between

January and February, she chose to spend one of those weeks at the City of Restoration, where she is a major financial sponsor. She enjoyed her stay so much that she has a standing commitment at the City of Restoration.

Unfortunately, Greg and Patricia Harris were unable to work out their differences and are no longer married. Patricia was re-elected as the Attorney General for the State of Texas. She lives in Austin with her children. I am looking forward to seeing her this year. She and Greg both tried very hard to make their marriage work. Although she forgave him, the pain and betrayal were too hard for Patricia to overcome. They stayed in the marriage for a year after our holiday celebration, and we could see their efforts. They really tried to keep it together, at least for the children's sake, but she came to the conclusion that their marriage was not a healthy example for their children, and she wanted a chance at true love. They both acknowledged that separation would be best for them and their children. They parted friends and continue to stay in communication with one another. Pastor Greg, although he remains single, continues to pastor his church.

Plessey and Alonzo Humphrey are still married, and the church is flourishing. Larkita is no longer a member of the church. Her son moved to Arizona, and she decided to move with him. Plessey continued to show love toward Larkita before she left. The church blended into a beautiful family.

What brings my heart such joy is the new relationship I have with Carla, Jane's daughter. She has taken a job at the

University of Miami, attends Ron's church, and is extremely active in the ministry. She has brought her gift of teaching to the Sunday School department, and the children are even more excited about children's church. I overheard an eight-year-old boy ministering to his six-year-old sister last week, and it touched my soul to the degree that it brought tears to my eyes. Last year, the same child was the main source of distraction in class, and his parents were coming to me for counseling with regards to his behavior at home. Under Carla's tutelage, the boy has blossomed into a little preacher. Carla is so much like her mother – she has even taken on Jane's habit of sitting in different places in and around the sanctuary each Sunday. She has brought so much life back into the church. It has helped heal the hearts of the people. She has helped many work through the grieving process. Her brothers and sisters have rallied around her, and she is now part of the family.

This year, pastors Larry and Terri Jones, Elona Braggs, Patricia Harris, Alonzo and Plessey Hutchins, all of their children – little ones and grown ones – and Ron Steinbeck and all of his children will be attending the Celebration honoring the life of Jane Steinbeck.

My immediate family is still struggling with the fragile balance we found when we first learned of Jake's lifestyle. Our expressions of continued support and love still at times get lost in the wake of the disciplinary action we had to take. Due to our actions to expose those in leadership who were not applying Godly principles to their lives, we lost a few of our key musicians, but some members who had been struggling have been delivered. This helped Jake to feel more comfortable with the decisions we made toward him. Although it hasn't been a smooth transition, Jake got an opportunity to witness first-hand the work of God's miraculous hand when dealing with homosexuality. He now feels assured that this is not a permanent condition, and that his life can change. We are continuing to pray for his deliverance.

In some ways, my life is richer because of Jane's decision. This in no way makes me miss her less, or would cause me to choose this over having her in my life, but I see the blessings that I might have overlooked had her death not awakened me to the fragility of a life empty of forgiveness. I am also more sensitive to those that are hurting, and I am more likely to reach out to that person instead of 'giving them their own space.' The consequences are too great, and life is too short to allow the ones we love to struggle when we can help them.

THE END